J. Allan Dunn

A Man to His Mate
(Action Thriller)

OK Publishing 2021

J. Allan Dunn

A Man to His Mate

(Action Thriller)

Treasure Hunt Thriller

Published by

MUSAICUM

Books

- Advanced Digital Solutions & High-Quality book Formatting -

musaicumbooks@okpublishing.info

2021 OK Publishing

ISBN 978-80-272-7590-8

Contents

CHAPTER I
BLIND SAMSON

It was perfect weather along the San Francisco water-front, and Rainey reacted to the brisk touch of the trade-wind upon his cheek, the breeze tempering the sun, bringing with it a tang of the open sea and a hint of Oriental spices from the wharves. He whistled as he went, watching a lumber coaster outward bound. The dull thump of a heavy cane upon the timbered walk and the shuffle of uncertain feet warned him from blundering into a man tapping his way along the Embarcadero, a giant who halted abruptly and faced him, leaning on the heavy stick.

"Matey," asked the giant, "could you put a blind man in the way of finding the sealin' schooner *Karluk*?"

The voice fitted its owner, Rainey thought — a basso voice tempered to the occasion, a deep-sea voice that could bellow above the roar of a gale if needed. For all his shoregoing clothes and shuffle, the man was certainly a sailor, or had been. All the skin uncovered by cloth or hair was weathered to leather, the great hands curled in as if they clutched an invisible rope. He wore dark glasses with side lenses, over which heavy brows projected in shaggy wisps of red hair.

Blind as the man proclaimed himself with voice and action, Rainey sensed something back of those colored glasses that seemed to be appraising him, almost as if the will of the man was peering, or listening, focused through those listless sockets. A kind of magnetism, not at all attractive, Rainey decided, even as he offered help and information.

"You're not fifty yards from the *Karluk*," Rainey replied. "But you're bound in the wrong direction. Let me put you right. I'm going that way myself."

"That's kind of ye, matey," said the other. "But I picked ye for that sort, hearin' you whistlin' as you came swingin' along. Light-hearted, I thinks, an' young, most likely; he'll help a stranded man. Give me the touch of yore arm, matey, an' I'll stow this spar of mine."

He swung about, slinging the curving handle of the stick over his right elbow as the fingers of his left hand placed themselves on Rainey's proffered arm. Strong fingers, almost vibrant with a force manifest through serge and linen. Fingers that could grip like steel upon occasion.

Rainey wonderingly sized up his consort. The stranger's bulk was enormous. Rainey was well over the average himself, but he was only a stripling beside this hulk, this stranded hulk, of manhood. And, for all the spectacled eyes and shuffling feet, there was a stamp of coordinated strength about the giant that bespoke the blind Samson. Given eyes, Rainey could imagine him agile as a panther, strong as a bear.

His weight was made up of thews and sinews, spare and solid flesh without an ounce of waste, upon a mighty skeleton. His face was heavy-bearded in hair of flaming, curling red, from high cheek-bones down out of sight below the soft loose collar of his shirt. The bridge of his glasses rested on the outcurve of a nose like the beak of an osprey, the ends of the wires looped about ears that lay close to the head, hairy about the inner-curves, lobeless, the tips suggesting the ear-tips of a satyr.

Mouth and jaw were hidden, but the beard could not deny the bold projection of the latter. About thirty, Rainey judged him. Buffeted by time and weather, but in the prime of his strength.

"Snow-blinded, matey," said the man. "North o' Point Barrow, a year an' more ago. Brought me up all standin'. What are you? Steamer man? Purser, maybe?"

"Newspaperman," answered Rainey. "Water-front detail. For the *Times*."

"You don't say so, matey? A writer, eh?"

Again Rainey felt the tug of that something back of the dark lenses, some speculation going on in the man's mind concerning him. And he felt the firm fingers contract ever so slightly, sinking into the muscles of his forearm for a second with a hint of how they could bruise and paralyze at will. Once more a faint sense of revulsion fought with his natural inclination to aid the handicapped mariner, and he shook it off.

"The *Karluk* sails to-morrow," he said.

"Aye, so — so they told me, matey. You've bin aboard?"

"I had a short talk with Captain Simms when she docked. Not much of a yarn. She didn't have a good trip, you know."

"Why, I didn't know. But — hold hard a minnit, will ye? You see, Simms is an old shipmate of mine. He don't dream I'm within a hundred miles o' here. Aye, or a thousand." He gave a deep-chested chuckle. "Now, then, matey, look here."

Rainey was anchored by the compelling grip. They stood next to the slip in which the sealer lay. The *Karluk's* decks were deserted, though there was smoke coming from the galley stovepipe.

"Simms is likely to be aboard," went on the other. "Ye see, I know his ways. An' I've come a long trip to see him. Nigh missed him. Only got in from Seattle this mornin'. He ain't expectin' me, an' it's in my mind to surprise him. By way of a joke. I don't want to be announced, ye see. Just drop in on him. How's the deck? Clear?"

"No one in sight," said Rainey.

"Fine! Mates an' crew down the Barb'ry Coast, I reckon. Sealers have liberties last shore-day. Like whalers. I've buried a few irons myself, matey, but I'll never sight the vapor of a right whale ag'in. Stranded, I am. So you'll do me a favor, matey, an' pilot me down into the cabin, if so be the skipper's there. If he ain't, I'll wait for him. I've got the right an' run o' the *Karluk's* cabin. I know ev'ry inch of her. You'll see when we go aboard. Let's go."

Rainey led him down the gangway to the deck of the sealer, still cluttered a bit with unstowed gear. Once on board, the blind man seemed to walk with assurance, guiding himself with touches here and there that showed his familiarity with the vessel's rig. And he no longer shuffled, but walked lightly, grinning at Rainey through his beard, with one blunt forefinger set to his mouth as he approached the cabin skylight, lifted on the port side. Through it came the murmur of voices. The blind man nodded in satisfaction and widened his grin with a warning "hush-h" to his guide.

"We'll fool 'em proper," he lipped rather than uttered.

The companion doors were closed, but they opened noiselessly. The stairs were carpeted with corrugated rubber that muffled all sound. Two men sat at the cabin table, leaning forward, hands and forearms outstretched, fingering something. One Rainey recognized as the captain, Simms — a heavy, square-built man, gray-haired, clean-shaven, his flesh tanned, yet somehow unhealthy, as if the bronze was close to tarnishing. There were deep puffs under the gray tired eyes.

The other was younger, tall, nervously active, with dark eyes and a dark mustache and beard, the latter trimmed to a Vandyke. Between them was a long slim sack of leather, a miner's poke. It was half full of something that stuffed its lower extremity solid, without doubt the same substance that glistened in the mouth of the sack and the palms of the two men — gold — coarse dust of gold!

Rainey felt himself thrust to one side as the blind man straddled across the bottom of the companionway, towering in the cabin while he thrust his stick with a thump on the floor and thundered, in a bellow that seemed to fill the place and come tumbling back in deafening echo:

"*Karluk* ahoy!"

The face of Captain Simms paled, the tan turned to a sickly gray, and his jaw dropped. Rainey saw fear come into his eyes. His companion did not stir a muscle except for the quick shift of his glance, but went on sitting at the table, the gold in one palm, the fingers of his other hand resting on the grains.

"Jim Lund!" gasped the captain hoarsely.

"That's me, you skulking sculpin? Thought I was bear meat by this, didn't you, blast yore rotten soul to hell! But I'm back, Bill Simms. Back, an' this time you don't slip me!"

Jim Lund's face was purple-red with rage, great veins standing out upon it so swollen that it seemed they must surely burst and discharge their congested contents. Out of the purpling flesh his scarlet hair curled in diabolical effect. His teeth gleamed through his beard, strong, yellow, far apart. He looked, Rainey thought, like a blind Berserker, restrained only by his affliction.

"You left me blind on the floe, Bill Simms!" he roared. "Blind, in a drivin' blizzard with the ice breakin' up! If I didn't have use for yore carcass I'd twist yore head from yore scaly body like I'd pull up a carrot."

Lund's fingers opened and closed convulsively. Before Rainey the vision of the threatened crime rose clear.

"I looked for you, Jim," pleaded the captain, and to Rainey his words lacked conviction. "I didn't know you were blind. I heard you shout just before the blizzard broke loose."

Lund answered with an inarticulate roar.

"And there's others present, Jim. I can explain it to you when we're by ourselves. When you're a mite calmer, Jim."

Lund banged his stick down on the table with a smashing blow that made the man with the Vandyke beard, still silent, keenly observant, draw back his arm with a catlike swiftness that only just evaded the stroke. The heavy wood landed fairly on the filled half of the poke and caused some of the gold to leap out of the mouth.

"What's that I hit?" asked Lund. "Soft, like a rat." He lunged forward, felt for the poke, and found it, lifted it, hefted it, his forehead puckered with deep seams, discovered the open end, poured out some of the colors on one palm, and used that for a mortar, grinding at the grains with his finger for a pestle, still weighing the stuff with a slight up-and-down movement of his hand.

He nodded as he slipped the poke into a side pocket, and the cabin grew very silent. Lund's face was grimly terrible. Rainey could have gone when the blind man reached for the gold and left the ladder clear. He had meant to go at the first opportunity, but now he was held fascinated by what was about to happen, and Lund stepped back across the companionway.

"So," said Lund, his deep voice muffled by some swift restraint. "You found it. And yo're going back after more?" His forehead was still creased with puzzlement. "Wal, I'm going with ye, eyes or no eyes, an' I'll keep tabs on ye, Bill Simms, by day and night. You can lay to that, you slimy-hearted swab!"

His voice had risen again. Rainey saw the sweat standing out on the captain's forehead as he answered:

"Of course you'll come, Jim. No need for you to talk this way."

"No need to talk! By the eternal, what I've got to say's bin steamin' in me for fourteen months o' blackness, an' it's comin' out, now it's started! Who's this man, who was talkin' with ye when I come aboard?"

He wheeled directly toward the man with the Vandyke, who still sat motionless, apparently calm, looking on as if at a play that might turn out to be either comedy or tragedy.

"That's Doctor Carlsen. He's to be surgeon this trip, Jim," said Simms deprecatingly, though he darted a look at Rainey half suspicious, half resentful.

Rainey, on the hint, turned toward the ladder quietly enough, but Lund had nipped him by the biceps before Rainey had taken a step.

"You'll stay right here," said Lund, "while I tell you an' this Doc Carlsen what kind of a man Simms is, with his poke full of gold and me with the price of my last meal spent two hours ago. I won't spin out the yarn.

"I rescued an Aleut off a bit of a berg one time. There warn't much of him left to rescue. Hands an' feet an' nose was frozen so he lost 'em, but the pore devil was grateful, an' he told me something. Told about an island north of Bering Strait, west of Kotzebue Sound, where there was gold on the beach richer and thicker than it ever lay at Nome. I makes for it, gits close enough for my Aleut to recognize it — it ain't an easy place to forget for one who has eyes — an' then we're blown south, an' we git into ice an' trouble. The Aleut dies, an' I lose my ship. But I was close enough to get the reckonin' of that island.

”Finally I land at Seattle, broke. I meet up with the man they call Hardluck Simms. Also they called him Honest Simms those days. Some said his honesty accounted for his hard luck. I like him, an' I finally tell him about my island. I put up the reckonin', an' he supplies the *Karluk*, grub, an' crew.

”Simms' luck is still ag'in' him. The *Karluk* gits into ice, gits nipped an' carried north, 'way north, with wind an' current, frozen tight in a floe. It looks like we've got to winter there. Mind ye, I've given Honest Simms the reckonin' of the island. We go out on the ice after bear, though the weather's threatenin', for we're short of meat. An' we kill a Kadiak bear. Me — I'll never stand for the shootin' of another bear if I can stop it.

”I've bin havin' trouble with my eyes. Right along. I'm on the floe not eighty yards from Simms. No, not sixty! It was me killed the bear, an' we're goin' back to the schooner for a sled. I stayed behind to bleed the brute. All of a sudden, like it always hits you, snow-blindness gits me, an' I shouts to Honest Simms. I'm blind, with my eyeballs on fire, an' the fire burnin' back inter my brain.

“Along comes a Point Arrow blister. That's a gale that breeds an' bursts of a second out of nowhere. It gathers up all the loose snow an' ice crystals an' drives 'em in a whirlwind. Presently the wind starts the ice to buckin' an' tremblin' like a jelly under you, splitting inter lanes. You lose yore direction even when you got eyes. I'm left in it by that bilge-blooded skunk, blind on the rockin', breakin' floe, while he scuds back to the schooner with his men. That's Honest Simms! Jim Lund's left behind but Honest Simms has the position of the island.”

“I didn't hear you call out you were blind, Lund. The wind blew your words away. I didn't know but what you were as right as the rest of us. The gale shut us all out from each other. We found the schooner by sheer luck before we perished. We looked for you — but the floe was broken up. We looked — ”

“Shut up!” bellowed Lund. ”You sailed inside of twenty-four hours, Honest Simms. The natives told me so later, when I could understand talk ag'in. D'ye know what saved me? The bear! I stumbled over the carcass when I was nigh spent. I ripped it up and clawed some of the warm guts, an' climbed inside the bloody body an' stayed there till it got cold an' clamped down over me. Waitin' for you to come an' git me, Honest Simms!

”That bear was bed and board to me until the natives found it, an' me in it, more dead than alive. Never mind the rest. I get here the day before you start back for more gold.

“An' I'm goin' with you. But first I'm goin' to have a full an' fair accountin' o' what you got already. I've got this young chap with me, an' he'll give me a hand to'ard a square deal.”

Lund propelled Rainey forward a few steps and then loosened his grip. The captain of the *Karluk* appealed to him directly.

”You're with the *Times*,” he said. All through the talk Rainey was conscious of the gaze of Doctor Carlsen, whose dark eyes appeared to be mocking the whole proceedings, looking on with the air of a man watching card-play with a prevision of how the game will come out.

“Mr. Lund is unstrung,” said the captain. ”He is under the delusion that we deliberately deserted him and, later, found the gold he speaks of. The first charge is nonsense. We did all that was possible in the frightful weather. We barely saved the ship.

“As for the gold, we touched on the island, and we did some prospecting, a very little, before we were driven offshore. The dust in the poke is all we secured. We are going back for more, quite naturally. I can prove all this to you by the log. It is manifestly not doctored, for we imagined Mr. Lund dead. If we had been able to work the beach thoroughly, nothing would tempt me into going back again to add to even a moderate fortune.”

Lund had been standing with his great head thrust forward as if concentrating all his remaining senses in an attempt to judge the captain's talk. The doctor sat with one leg crossed, smoking a cigarette, his expression sardonic, sphinxlike. To Rainey, a little bewildered at being dragged into the affair, and annoyed at it, Captain Simms' words rang true enough. He did not know what to say, whether to speak at all. Lund supplied the gap.

"If that ain't the truth, you lie well, Simms," he said. "But I don't trust ye. You lie when you say you didn't hear me call out I was blind. Sixty yards away, I was, an' the wind hadn't started. I was afraid — yes, afraid — an' I yelled at the top of my lungs. An' you sailed off inside of twenty-four hours."

"Driven off."

"I don't believe ye. You deserted me — left me blind, tucked in the bloody, freezin' carcass of a bear. Left me like the cur you are. Why, you — "

The rising frenzy of Lund's voice was suddenly broken by the clear note of a girl's voice. One of two doors in the after-end of the main cabin had opened, and she stood in the gap, slim, yellow-haired, with gray eyes that blazed as they looked on the little tableau.

"Who says my father is a cur?" she demanded. "You?" And she faced Lund with such intrepid challenge in her voice, such stinging contempt, that the giant was silenced.

"I was dressing," she said, "or I would have come out before. If you say my father deserted you, you lie!"

Captain Simms turned to her. Doctor Carlsen had risen and moved toward her. Rainey wished he was on the dock. Here was a story breaking that was a *saga* of the North. He did not want to use it, somehow. The girl's entrance, her vivid, sudden personality forbade that. He felt an intruder as her eyes regarded him, standing by Lund's side in apparent sympathy with him, arrayed against her father. And yet he was not certain that Lund had not been betrayed. The remembrance of the first look in the captain's face when he had glanced up from handling the gold and seen Lund was too keen.

"Go into your cabin, Peggy," said the captain. "This is no place for you. I can handle the matter. Lund has cause for excitement; but I can satisfy him."

Lund stood frozen, like a pointer on scent, all his faculties united in attention toward the girl. To Rainey he seemed attempting to visualize her by sheer sense of hearing, by perceptions quickened in the blind. The doctor crossed to the girl and spoke to her in a low voice.

Lund spoke, and his voice was suddenly mild.

"I didn't know there was a lady present, miss," he said. "Yore father's right. You let us settle this. We'll come to an agreement."

But, for all his swift change to placability, there was a sinister undertone to his voice that the girl seemed to recognize. She hesitated until her father led her back into the cabin.

"You two'll sit down?" said the doctor, speaking aloud for the first time, his voice amiable, carefully neutral. "And we'll have a drop of something. Mr. Lund, I can understand your attitude. You've suffered a great deal. But you have misunderstood Captain Simms. I have heard about this from him, before. He has no desire to cheat you. He is rejoiced to see you alive, though afflicted. He is still Honest Simms, Mr. Lund.

"I haven't your name, sir," he went on pleasantly, to Rainey. "The captain said you were a newspaperman?"

"John Rainey, of the *Times*. I knew nothing of this before I came aboard."

"And you will understand, of course, what Mr. Lund overlooked in his natural agitation, that this is not a story for your paper. We should have a fleet trailing us. We must ask your confidence, Mr. Rainey."

There was a strong personality in the doctor, Rainey realized. Not the blustering, driving force of Lund, but a will that was persistent, powerful. He did not like the man from first appearances. He was too aloof, too sardonic in his attitudes. But his manner was friendly enough, his voice compelling in its suggestion that Rainey was a man to be trusted. Captain Simms came back into the cabin, closing the door of his daughter's room.

"We are going to have a little drink together," said the doctor. "I have some Scotch in my cabin. If you'll excuse me for a moment? Captain, will you get some glasses, and a chair for Mr. Lund?"

The captain looked at Rainey a little uncertainly, and then at Lund, whose aggressiveness seemed to have entirely departed. It was Rainey who got the chair for the latter and seated himself. He would join in a friendly drink and then be well shut of the matter, he told himself.

And he would promise not to print the story, or talk of it. That was rotten newspaper craft, he supposed, but he was not a first-class man, in that sense. He let his own ethics interfere sometimes with his pen and what the paper would deem its best interests. And this was a whale of a yarn.

But it was true that its printing would mean interference with the *Karluk's* expedition. And there was the girl. Rainey was not going to forget the girl. If the *Karluk* ever came back? But then she would be an heiress.

Rainey pulled himself up for a fool at the way his thoughts were racing as the doctor came back with a bottle of Scotch whisky and a siphon. The captain had set out glasses and a pitcher of plain water from a rack.

"I imagine you'll be the only one who'll take seltzer, Mr. Rainey," said the doctor pleasantly, passing the bottle. "Captain Simms, I know, uses plain water. Siphons are scarce at sea. I suppose Mr. Lund does the same. And I prefer a still drink."

"Plain water for mine," said Lund.

"We're all charged," said the doctor. "Here's to a better understanding!"

"Glad to see you aboard, Mr. Rainey," said the captain.

Lund merely grunted.

Rainey took a long pull at his glass. The cabin was hot, and he was thirsty. The seltzer tasted a little flat — or the whisky was of an unusual brand, he fancied. And then inertia suddenly seized him. He lost the use of his limbs, of his tongue, when he tried to call out. He saw the doctor's sardonic eyes watching him as he strove to shake off a lethargy that swiftly merged into dizziness.

Dimly he heard the scrape of the captain's chair being pushed back. From far off he heard Lund's big voice booming, "Here, what's this?" and the doctor's cutting in, low and eager; then he collapsed, his head falling forward on his outstretched arms.

CHAPTER II
A DIVIDED COMPANY

It was not the first time that Rainey had been on a ship, a sailing ship, and at sea. Whenever possible his play-hours had been spent on a little knockabout sloop that he owned jointly with another man, both of them members of the Corinthian Club. While the *Curlew* had made no blue-water voyages, they had sailed her more than once up and down the California coast on offshore regattas and pleasure-trips, and, lacking experience in actual navigation, Rainey was a pretty handy sailorman for an amateur.

So, as he came out of the grip of the drug that had been given him, slowly, with a brain-pan that seemed overstuffed with cotton and which throbbed with a dull persistent ache — with a throat that seemed to be coated with ashes, strangely contracted — a nauseated stomach — eyes that saw things through a haze — limbs that ached as if bruised — the sounds that beat their way through his sluggish consciousness were familiar enough to place him almost instantly and aid his memory's flickering film to reel off what had happened.

As he lay there in a narrow bunk, watching the play of light that came through a porthole beyond his line of vision, noting in this erratic shuttling of reflected sunlight the roll and pitch of cabin walls, listening to the low boom of waves followed by the swash alongside that told him the *Karluk* was bucking heavy seas, a slow rage mastered him, centered against the doctor with the sardonic smile and Captain Simms, who Rainey felt sure had tacitly approved of the doctor's actions.

He remembered Lund's exclamation of, "Here, what's this?" — the question of a blind man who could not grasp what was happening — and acquitted him.

They had deliberately kidnapped him, shanghaied him, because they did not choose to trust him, because they thought he might print the story of the island treasure beach in his paper, or babble of it and start a rush to the new strike of which he had seen proof in the gold dust streaming from the poke.

He had been willing to suppress the yarn, Rainey reflected bitterly, his intentions had been fair and square in this situation forced upon him, and they had not trusted him. They were taking no chances, he thought, and suddenly wondered what position the girl would take in the matter. He could not think of her approving it. Yet she would naturally side with her father, as she had done against Lund's accusations. And Rainey suspected that there was something back of Lund's charge of desertion. The girl's face, her graceful figure, the tones of her voice, clung in his still palsied recollection a long time before he could dismiss it and get round to the main factor of his imprisonment — *what were they going to do with him?*

There was a fortune in sight. For gold, men forget the obligations of life and law in civilization; they revert to savage type, and their minds and actions are swayed by the primitive urge of lust. Treachery, selfishness, cruelty, crime breed from the shining particles even before they are in actual sight and touch.

Rainey knew that. He had read many true yarns that had come down from the frozen North, in from the deserts and the mountains, tales of the mining records of the West.

He mistrusted the doctor. The man had drugged him. He was a man whose profession, where the mind was warped, belittled life. Captain Simms had been charged with leaving a blind man on a broken floe. Lund was the type whose passions left him ruthless. The crew — they would be bound by shares in the enterprise, a rough lot, daring much and caring little for anything beyond their own narrow horizons. The girl was the only redeeming feature of the situation.

Was it because of her — it might be because of her special pleading — that they had not gone further? Or were they still fighting through the heads, waiting until they got well out to sea before they disposed of him, so there would be no chance of his telltale body washing up along the coast for recognition and search for clues? He wondered whether any one had seen him go aboard the *Karluk* with Lund — any one who would remember it and mention the circumstance when he was found to be missing.

That might take a day or two. At the office they would wonder why he didn't show up to cover his detail, because he had been steady in his work. But they would not suspect foul play at first. He had no immediate family. His landlady lodged other newspapermen, and was used to their vagaries. And all this time the *Karluk* would be thrashing north, well out to sea, unsighted, perhaps, for all her trip, along that coast of fogs.

Rainey had disappeared, dropped out of sight. He would be a front-page wonder for a day, then drop to paragraphs for a day or so more, and that would be the end of it.

But they had made him comfortable. He was not in a smelly forecastle, but in a bunk in a cabin that must open off the main room of the schooner. Why had they treated him with such consideration? He dozed off, for all his wretchedness, exhausted by his efforts to untangle the snarl. When he awoke again his mouth was glued together with thirst.

The schooner was still fighting the sea — the wind, too, Rainey fancied — sailing close-hauled, going north against the trade. He fumbled for his watch. It had run down. His head ached intolerably. Each hair seemed set in a nerve center of pain. But he was better.

Back of his thirst lay hunger now, and the apathy that had held him to idle thinking had given way to an energy that urged him to action and discovery.

As he sat up in his bunk, fully clothed as he had come aboard, the door of his cabin opened and the doctor appeared, nodded coolly as he saw Rainey moving, disappeared for an instant, and brought in a draft of some sort in a long glass.

"Take this," said Carlsen. "Pull you together. Then we'll get some food into you."

The calm insolence of the doctor's manner, ignoring all that had happened, seemed to send all the blood in Rainey's body fuming to his brain. He took the glass and hurled its contents at Carlsen's face. The doctor dodged, and the stuff splashed against the cabin wall, only a few drops reaching Carlsen's coat, which he wiped off with his handkerchief, unruffled.

"Don't be a damned fool," he said to Rainey, his voice irritatingly even. "Are you afraid it's drugged? I would not be so clumsy. I could have given you a hypodermic while you slept, enough to keep you unconscious for as many hours as I choose — or forever.

"I'll mix you another dose — one more — take it or leave it. Take it, and you'll soon feel yourself again after Tamada has fed you. Then we'll thrash out the situation. Leave it, and I wash my hands of you. You can go for'ard and bunk with the men and do the dirty work."

He spoke with the calm assumption of one controlling the schooner, Rainey noted, rather as skipper than surgeon. But Rainey felt that he had made a fool of himself, and he took the second draft, which almost instantly relieved him, cleansing his mouth and throat and, as his headache died down, clearing his brain.

"Why did you drug me?" he demanded. "Pretty high-handed. I can make you pay for this."

"Yes? How? When? We're well off Cape Mendocino, heading nor'west or thereabouts. Nothing between us and Unalaska but fog and deep water. Before we get back you'll see the payment in a different light. We're not pirates. This was plain business. A million or more in sight.

"Lund nearly spilled things as it was, raving the way he did. It's a wonder some one didn't overhear him with sense enough to tumble.

"We didn't take any chances. Rounded up the crew, and got out. The man who's made a gold discovery thinks everybody else is watching him. It's a genuine risk. If they followed us, they'd crowd us off the beach. I don't suppose any one has followed us. If they have, we've lost them in this fog.

"But we didn't take any risks after Lund's blowing off. He might have done it ashore before you brought him aboard. I don't think so. But he might. And so might you, later."

"I'd have given you my word."

"And meant to keep it. But you'd have been an uncertain factor, a weak link. You might have given it away in your sleep. You heard enough to figure the general locality of the island when Lund blurted it out. You knew too much. Suppose the *Karluk* fought up to Kotzebue Bay and found a dozen power-vessels hanging about, waiting for us to lead them to the beach? And we'd have worried all the way up, with you loose. You're a newspaperman. The suppression of this yarn would have obsessed you, lain on your reportorial conscience.

"I don't suppose your salary is much over thirty a week, is it? Now, then, here you are in for a touch of real adventure, better than gleaning dock gossip, to a red-blooded man. If we win — and you saw the gold — *you* win. We expect to give you a share. We haven't taken it up yet, but it'll be enough. More than you'd earn in ten years, likely, more than you'd be apt to save in a lifetime. We kidnapped you for your own good. You're a prisoner *de luxe*, with the run of the ship."

"I can work my passage," said Rainey. He could see the force of the doctor's argument, though he didn't like the man. He didn't trust the doctor, though he thought he'd play fair about the gold. But it was funny, his assuming control.

"Yachted a bit?" asked Carlsen.

"Yes."

"Can you navigate?"

Rainey thought he caught a hint of emphasis to this question.

"I can learn," he said. "Got a general idea of it."

"Ah!" The doctor appeared to dismiss the subject with some relief. "Well," he went on, "are you open to reason — and food? I'm sorry about your friends and folks ashore, but you're not the first prodigal who has come back with the fatted calf instead of hungry for it."

"That part of it is all right," said Rainey. There was no help for the situation, save to make the most of it and the best. "But I'd like to ask you a question."

"Go ahead. Have a cigarette?"

Rainey would rather have taken it from any one else, but the whiff of burning tobacco, as Carlsen lit up, gave him an irresistible craving for a smoke. Besides, it wouldn't do for the doctor to know he mistrusted him. If he was to be a part of the ship's life, there was small sense in acting pettishly. He took the cigarette, accepted the light, and inhaled gratefully.

"What's the question?" asked Carlsen.

"You weren't on the last trip. You weren't in on the original deal. But I find you doing all the talking, making me offers. You drugged me on your own impulse. Where's the skipper? How does he stand in this matter? Why didn't he come to see me? What is your rating aboard?"

"You're asking a good deal for an outsider, it seems to me, Rainey. I came to you partly as your doctor. But I speak for the captain and the crew. Don't worry about that."

"And Lund?" Rainey could not resist the shot. He had gathered that the doctor resented Lund.

Carlsen's eyes narrowed.

"Lund will be taken care of," he said, and, for the life of him, Rainey could not judge the statement for threat or friendly promise. "As for my status, I expect to be Captain Simms' son-in-law as soon as the trip is over."

"All right," said Rainey. Carlsen's announcement surprised him. Somehow he could not place the girl as the doctor's fiancée. "I suppose the captain may mention this matter," he queried, "to cement it?"

"He may," replied Carlsen enigmatically. "Feel like getting up?"

Rainey rose and bathed face and hands. Carlsen left the cabin. The main room was empty when Rainey entered, but there was a place set at the table. Through the skylight he noted, as he glanced at the telltale compass in the ceiling, that the sun was low toward the west.

The main cabin was well appointed in hardwood, with red cushions on the transoms and a creeping plant or so hanging here and there. A canary chirped up and broke into rolling song. It was all homy, innocuous. Yet he had been drugged at the same table not so long before. And now he was pledged a share of ungathered gold. It was a far cry back to his desk in the *Times* office.

A Japanese entered, sturdy, of white-clad figure, deft, polite, incurious. He had brought in some ham and eggs, strong coffee, sliced canned peaches, bread and butter. He served as Rainey ate heartily, feeling his old self coming back with the food, especially with the coffee.

"Thanks, Tamada," he said as he pushed aside his plate at last.

"Everything arright, sir?" purred the Japanese.

Rainey nodded. The "sir" was reassuring. He was accepted as a somebody aboard the *Karluk*. Tamada cleared away swiftly, and Rainey felt for his own cigarettes. He hesitated a little to smoke in the cabin, thinking of the girl, wondering whether she was on deck, where he intended to go. Some one was snoring in a stateroom off the cabin, and he fancied by its volume it was Lund.

It was a divided ship's company, after all. For he knew that Lund, handicapped with his blindness, would live perpetually suspicious of Simms. And the doctor was against Lund. Rainey's own position was a paradox.

He started for the companionway, and a slight sound made him turn, to face the girl. She looked at him casually as Rainey, to his annoyance, flushed.

"Good afternoon," said Rainey. "Are you going on deck?"

It was not a clever opening, but she seemed to rob him of wit, to an extent. He had yet to know how she stood concerning his presence aboard. Did she countenance the forcible kidnapping of him as a possible tattler? Or — ?

"My father tells me you have decided to go with us," she said, pleasantly enough, but none too cordially, Rainey thought.

"Doctor Carlsen helped me to my decision."

She did not seem to regard this as a thrust, but stood lightly swaying to the pitch of the vessel, regarding him with grave eyes of appraisal.

"You have not been well," she said. "I hope you are better. Have you eaten?"

Rainey began to think that she was ignorant of the facts. And he made up his mind to ignore them. There was nothing to be gained by telling her things against her father — much less against her fiancée, the doctor.

"Thank you, I have," he said. "I was going to look up Mr. Lund."

The sentence covered a sudden change of mind. He no longer wanted to go on deck with the girl. They were not to be intimates. She was to marry Carlsen. He was an outsider. Carlsen had told him that. So she seemed to regard him, impersonally, without interest. It piqued him.

"Mr. Lund is in the first mate's cabin," said the girl, indicating a door. "Mr. Bergstrom, who was mate, died at sea last voyage. Doctor Carlsen acts as navigator with my father, but he has another room."

She passed him and went on deck. Carlsen was acting first mate as well as surgeon. That meant he had seamanship. Also that they had taken in no replacements, no other men to swell the little corporation of fortune-hunters who knew the secret, or a part of it. It was unusual, but Rainey shrugged his shoulders and rapped on the door of the cabin.

It took loud knocking to waken Lund. At last he roared a "Come in."

Rainey found him seated on the edge of his bunk, dressed in his underclothes, his glasses in place. Rainey wondered whether he slept in them. Lund's uncanny intuition seemed to read the thought. He tapped the lenses.

"Hate to take them off," he said. "Light hurts my eyes, though the optic nerve is dead. Seems to strike through. How're ye makin' out?"

Rainey gave Lund the full benefit of his blindness. The giant could not have known what was in the doctor's mind, but he must have learned something. Lund was not the type to be satisfied with half answers, and undoubtedly felt that he held a proprietary interest in the *Karluk* by virtue of his being the original owner of the secret. Rainey wondered if he had sensed the doctor's attitude in that direction, an attitude expressed largely by the expression of Carlsen's face, always wearing the faint shadow of a sneer.

"You know they drugged me," Rainey ended his recital of the interview he had had with the doctor.

"Knockout drops? I guessed it. That doctor's slick. Well, you've not much fault to find, have ye? Carlsen talked sense. Here you are on the road to a fortune. I'll see yore share's a fair one. There's plenty. It ain't a bad billet you've fallen into, my lad. But I'll look out for ye. I'm sort of responsible for yore trip, ye see, matey. And I'll need ye."

He lowered his voice mysteriously.

"Yo're a writer, Mister Rainey. You've got brains. You can see which way a thing's heading. You've heard enough. I'm blind. I've bin done dirt once aboard the *Karluk*, and I don't aim to stand for it ag'in. And I had my eyes, then. No use livin' in a rumpus. Got to keep watch. Got to keep yore eyes open.

"And I ain't got eyes. You have. Use 'em for both of us. I ain't asking ye to take sides, exactly. But I've got cause for bein' suspicious. I don't call the skipper *Honest* Simms no more. And I ain't stuck on that doctor. He's too bossy. He's got the skipper under his thumb. And there's somethin' funny about the skipper. Notice ennything?"

"Why, I don't know him," said Rainey. "He doesn't look extra well, what I've seen of him. Only the once."

"He's logey," said Lund confidentially. "He ain't the same man. Mebbe it's his conscience. But that doctor's runnin' him."

"He's going to marry the captain's daughter," said Rainey.

"Simms' daughter? Carlsen goin' to marry her? Ump! That may account for the milk in the cocoanut. She's a stranger to me. Lived ashore with her uncle and aunt, they tell me. Carlsen was the family doctor. Now she's off with her father."

His face became crafty, and he reached out for Rainey's knee, found it as readily as if he had sight, and tapped it for emphasis.

"That makes all the more reason for us lookin' out for things, matey," he went on, almost in a whisper. "If they've played me once they may do it ag'in. And they've got the odds, settin' aside my eyes. But I can turn a trick or two. You an' me come aboard together. You give me a hand. Stick to me, an' I'll see you git yore whack.

"I'll have yore bunk changed. You'll come in with me. An' we'll put one an' one together. We'll be mates. Treat 'em fair if they treat us fair. But don't forget they fixed yore grog. I had nothin' to do with that. I may be stranded, but, if the tide rises — "

He set the clutch of his powerful fingers deep into Rainey's leg above the knee with a grip that left purple bruises there before the day was over.

"We two, matey," he said. "Now you an' me'll have a tot of stuff that ain't doped."

He moved about the little cabin with an astounding freedom and sureness, chuckling as he handled bottle and glasses and measured out the whisky and water.

"W'en yo're blind," he said, ramming his pipe full of black tobacco, "they's other things comes to ye. I know the run of this ship, blindfold, you might say. I c'ud go aloft in a pinch, or steer her. More grog?"

But Rainey abstained after the first glass, though Lund went on lowering the bottle without apparent effect.

"So yo're a bit of a sailor?" the giant asked presently. "An' a scholar. You can navigate, I make no doubt?"

"I hope to get a chance to learn on the trip," answered Rainey. "I know the general principles, but I've never tried to use a sextant. I'm going to get the skipper to help me out. Or Carlsen."

"Carlsen! What in hell does a doctor know about navigation?" demanded Lund.

Rainey told him what the girl had said, and the giant grunted.

"I have my doubts whether they'll ever help ye," he said. "Wish I could. But it 'ud be hard without my eyes. An' I've got no sextant an' no book o' tables. It's too bad."

His disappointment seemed keen, and Rainey could not fathom it. Why had both Lund and Carlsen seemed to lay stress on this matter? Why was the doctor relieved and Lund disappointed at his ignorance?

As they came out of the stateroom together, later, Lund reeking of the liquor he had absorbed, though remaining perfectly sober, his hand laid on Rainey's shoulder, perhaps for guidance but with a show of familiarity, Rainey saw the girl looking at him with a glance in which contempt showed unveiled. It was plain that his intimacy with Lund was not going to advance him in her favor.

CHAPTER III
TARGET PRACTISE

The *Karluk* was an eighty-five-ton schooner, Gloster Fisherman type, with a length of ninety and a beam of twenty-five feet. Her enormous stretch of canvas, spread to the limit on all possible occasions by Captain Simms, was offset by the pendulum of lead that made up her keel, and she could slide through the seas at twelve knots on her best point of sailing — reaching — the wind abaft her beam.

After Rainey had demonstrated at the wheel that he had the mastery of her and had shown that he possessed sea-legs, a fair amount of seacraft and, what the sailors did not possess, initiative, Captain Simms appointed him second mate.

"We don't carry one as a rule," the skipper said. "But it'll give you a rating and the right to eat in the cabin." He had not brought up the subject of Rainey's kidnapping, and Rainey let it go. There was no use arguing about the inevitable. The rating and the cabin fare seemed offered as an apology, and he was willing to accept it.

Carlsen acted as first mate, and Rainey had to acknowledge him efficient. He fancied the man must have been a ship's surgeon, and so picked up his seamanship. After a few days Carlsen, save for taking noon observations with the skipper and working out the reckoning, left his duties largely to Rainey, who was glad enough for the experience. A sailor named Hansen was promoted to acting-quartermaster, and relieved Rainey. Carlsen spent most of his time attendant on the girl or chatting with the hunters, with whom he soon appeared on terms of intimacy.

The hunters esteemed themselves above the sailors, as they were, in intelligence and earning capacity. The forecastlemen acted, on occasion, as boat-steerers and rowers for the hunters, each of whom had his own boat from which to shoot the cruising seals.

There were six hunters and twelve sailors, outside of a general roustabout and butt named "Sandy," who cleaned up the forecastle and the hunters' quarters, where they messed apart, and helped Tamada, the cook, in the galley with his pots and dishes. But now there was no work in prospect for the hunters, and they lounged on deck or in the 'midship quarters, spinning yarns or playing poker. They were after gold this trip, not seals.

"'Cordin' to the agreement," Lund said to Rainey, "the gold's to be split into a hundred shares. One for each sailorman, an' they chip in for the boy. Two for the hunters, two for the cook, four for Bergstrom, the first mate, who died at sea. Twenty for 'ship's share.' Fifty shares to be split between Simms an' me."

"What's the 'ship's share'?" asked Rainey.

"Represents capital investment. Matter of fact, it belongs to the gal," said Lund. "Simms gave her the *Karluk*. It's in her name with the insurance."

"Then he and his daughter get forty-five shares, and you only twenty-five?"

"You got it right," grinned Lund. "Simms is no philanthropist. It wa'n't so easy for me to git enny one to go in with me, son. I ain't the first man to come trailin' in with news of a strike. An' I had nothin' to show for it. Not even a color of gold. Nothin' but the word of a dead Aleut, my own jedgment, an' my own sight of an island I never landed on. Matter of fact, Honest Simms was the only one who didn't laff at me outright. It was on'y his bad luck made him try a chance at gold 'stead of keepin' after pelts.

"An' we had a hard an' tight agreement drawn up on paper, signed, witnessed an' recorded. 'Course it holds him as well as it holds me, but he gits the long end of *that* stick. W'en I read, or got it read to me, in the Seattle *News-Courier*, that the *Karluk* was listed as 'Arrived' in San Francisco, it was all I could do to git carfare an' grub money. If I hadn't bin blind, an' some of 'em half-way human to'ards a man with his lights out, I'd never have raised it. I'd have got here someways, matey, if I'd had to walk, but I'd have got here a bit late. Then I'd have had to wait till Simms got back ag'in — an' mebbe starved to death.

"But I'm here an' I've got some say-so. One thing, you're goin' to git Bergstrom's share. I don't give a damn where the doctor comes in. If he marries the gal he'll git her twenty shares, ennyway. Though he ain't married her yet. And I ain't through with Simms yet," he added, with an emphasis that was a trifle grim, Rainey thought.

"The crew, hunters an' sailors, don't seem over glad to see me back," Lund went on. "Mebbe they figgered their shares 'ud be bigger. Mebbe the doc's queered me. He's pussy-footin' about with 'em a good deal. But I'll talk with you about that later. It's me an' you ag'in' the rest of 'em, seems to me, Rainey. The doc's aimin' to be the Big Boss aboard this schooner. He's got the skipper buffaloed. But not me, not by a jugful."

He slammed his big fist against the side of the bunk so viciously that it seemed to jar the cabin. The blow was typical of the man, Rainey decided. He felt for Lund not exactly a liking, but an attraction, a certain compelled admiration. The giant was elemental, with a driving force inside him that was dynamic, magnetic. What a magnificent pirate he would have made, thought Rainey, looking at his magnificent proportions and considering the crude philosophies that cropped out in his talk.

"I'm in life for the loot of it, Rainey," Lund declared. "Food an' drink to tickle my tongue an' fill my belly, the woman I happen to want, an' bein' able to buy ennything I set my fancy on. The answer to that is Gold. With it you can buy most enny thing. Not all wimmen, I'll grant you that. Not the kind of woman I'd want for a steady mate. Thet's one thing I've found out can't be bought, my son, the honor of a good woman. An' thet's the sort of woman I'm lookin' for.

"I reckon yo're raisin' yore eyebrows at that?" he challenged Rainey. "But the other kind, that'll sell 'emselves, 'll sell you jest as quick — an' quicker. I'd wade through hell-fire hip-deep to git the right kind — an' to hold her. An' I'll buck all hell to git what's comin' to me in the way of luck, or go down all standin' tryin'. This is my gold, an' I'm goin' to handle it. If enny one tries to swizzle me out of it I'm goin' to swizzle back, an' you can lay to that. Not forgettin' them that stands by me."

Between Lund and Simms there existed a sort of armed truce. No open reference was made to the desertion of Lund on the floe. But Rainey knew that it rankled in Lund's mind. The five, Peggy Simms, her father, Carlsen, Lund and Rainey, ostensibly messed together, but Rainey's duties generally kept him on deck until Carlsen had sufficiently completed his own meal to relieve him. By that time the girl and the captain had left the table.

Lund invariably waited for Rainey. Tamada kept the food hot for them. And served them, Lund making good play with spoon or fork and a piece of bread, the Japanese cutting up his viands conveniently beforehand.

To Rainey, Tamada seemed the hardest worked man aboard ship. He had three messes to cook and he was busy from morning until night, efficient, tireless and even-tempered. The crew, though they acknowledged his skill, were Californians, either by birth or adoption, and the racial prejudice against the Japanese was apparent.

A week of good wind was followed by dirty weather. The *Karluk* proved a good fighter, though her headway was materially lessened by contrary wind and sea, and the persistence and increasing opposition of the storm seemed to have a corresponding effect upon Captain Simms.

He grew daily more irritable and morose, even to his daughter. Only the doctor appeared able to get along with him on easy terms, and Rainey noticed that, to Carlsen, the skipper seemed conciliatory even to deference.

Peggy Simms watched her father with worried eyes. The curious, tarnished look of his tanned skin grew until the flesh seemed continually dry and of an earthy color; his lips peeled, and more than once he shook as if with a chill.

On the eleventh day out, Rainey went below in the middle of the afternoon for his sea-boots. The gale had suddenly strengthened and, under reefs, the *Karluk* heeled far over until the hissing seas flooded the scuppers and creamed even with the lee rail. In the main cabin he found Simms seated in a chair with his daughter leaning over him, speaking to her in a harsh, complaining voice.

"No, you can't do a thing for me," he was saying. "It's this sciatica. I've got to get Carlsen."

As Rainey passed through to his own little stateroom neither of them noticed him, but he saw that the captain was shivering, his hands picking almost convulsively at the table-cloth.

"Where's Carlsen, curse him!" Rainey heard through his cabin partition. "Tell him I can't stand this any longer. He's got to help me. Got to. *Got to.*"

As Rainey appeared, walking heavily in his boots, the girl looked up. Her father was slumped in his chair, his face buried on his folded arms. The girl glanced at him doubtfully, apparently uncertain whether to go herself to find Carlsen or stay with her father.

"Anything I can do, Miss Simms? Your father seems quite ill."

The hesitation of the girl even to speak to him was very plain to Rainey. Suddenly she threw up her chin.

"Kindly find Doctor Carlsen," she ordered, rather than requested. "Ask him to come as soon as he can. I — " She turned uncertainly to her father.

"Can I help you to get him into the cabin?" asked Rainey.

She thanked him with lips, not eyes, and he assisted her to shift the almost helpless man into his room and bunk. He was like a stuffed sack between them, save that his body twitched. While Rainey took most of the weight, he marveled at the strength of the slender girl and the way in which she applied it. Simms seemed to have fainted, to be on the verge of unconsciousness or even utter collapse. Rainey felt his wrist, and the pulse was almost imperceptible.

"I'll get the doctor immediately," he said.

She nodded at him, chafing her father's hands, her own face pale, and a look of anxious fear in her eyes.

"Mighty funny sort of sciatica," Rainey told himself as he hurried forward. He knew where Carlsen was, in the hunters' cozy quarters, playing poker. From the chips in front of him he had been winning heavily.

"The skipper's ill," said Rainey. "No pulse. Almost unconscious."

Carlsen raised his eyebrows.

"Didn't know you were a physician," he said. "Just one of his spells. I'll finish this hand. Too good to lay down. The skipper can wait for once."

The hunters grinned as Carlsen took his time to draw his cards, make his bets and eventually win the pot on three queens.

"I wonder what your real game is?" Rainey asked himself as he affected to watch the play. According to his own announcement Carlsen was deliberately neglecting the father of the girl he was to marry and at the same time slighting the captain to his own men. Carlsen drew in his chips and leisurely made a note of the amount.

"Quite a while yet to settling-day," he said to the players. "Luck may swing all round the compass before then, boys. All right, Rainey, you needn't wait."

Rainey ignored the omitted "Mister." He held the respect of the sailors, since he had shown his ability, but he knew that the hunters regarded him with an amused tolerance that lacked disrespect by a small margin. To them he was only the amateur sailor. Rainey fancied that the doctor had contributed to this attitude, and it did not lessen his score against Carlsen.

The captain did not make his appearance for that day, the next, or the next. The men began to roll eyes at one another when they asked after his health. Carlsen kept his own counsel, and Peggy Simms spent most of her time in the main cabin with her eyes always roving to her father's door. Rainey noticed that Tamada brought no food for the sick man. Carlsen was the apparent controller of the schooner. Lund was quick to sense this.

"We got to block that Carlsen's game," he said to Rainey. "There's a nigger in the woodpile somewhere an' you an' me got to uncover him, matey, afore we reach Bering Strait, or you an' me'll finish this trip squattin' on the rocks of one of the Four Mountain Islands makin' faces at the gulls.

"I wish you c'ud git under the skin of that Jap. No use tryin' to git in with the crew or the hunters. They're ag'in' both of us — leastwise the hunters are. The hands don't count. They're jest plain hash."

Lund spoke with an absolute contempt of the sailors that was characteristic of the man.

"You think they'd put a blind man ashore that way?" asked Rainey.

"Carlsen would. In a minnit. He'd argy that you c'ud look out for me, seein' as we are chums. As for you, you've bin useful, but you can't navigate, an' you've helped train Hansen to yore work. You were in the way at the start, an' he'd jest as soon git rid of you that road as enny other. He don't intend you to have Bergstrom's share, by a jugful."

Lund grinned as he spoke, and Rainey felt a little chill raise gooseflesh all over his body. It was not exactly fear, but —

"They don't look on us two as *mascots*," went on Lund. "But to git back to that Jap. Forewarned is forearmed. He ain't over an' above liked, but they've got used to him goin' back an' forth with their grub, an' they sort of despise him for a yellow-skinned coolie.

"Now Tamada ain't no coolie. I know Japs. He's a cut above his job. Cooks well enough for a swell billet ashore if he wanted it. An' there ain't much goin' on that Tamada ain't wise to. See if you can't get next to him. Trubble is he's too damn' neutral. He knows he's safe, becoz he's cook an' a damn' good one. But he's wise to what Carlsen's playin' at.

"Carlsen don't care for man, woman, God, or the devil. Neither do I," he concluded. "An' I've got a card or two up my sleeve. But I'd sure like to git a peep at what the doc's holdin'."

The storm blew out, and there came a spell of pleasant weather, with the *Karluk* gliding along, logging a fair rate where a less well-designed vessel would barely have found steerage way, riding on an almost even keel. Simms was still confined to his cabin, though now his daughter took him in an occasional tray.

Except for observations and the details of navigation, Carlsen left the schooner to Rainey. They were well off the coast, out of the fogs, apparently alone upon the lonely ocean that ran sparkling to the far horizon. It was warm, there was little to do, the sailors, as well as the hunters, spent most of their time lounging on the deck.

Save at meal-times, Carlsen, for one who had announced himself as an accepted lover, neglected the girl, who had devoted herself to her father. Yet she seldom went into her cabin, never remained there long, and time must have hung heavily on her hands. A girl of her spirit must have resented such treatment, Rainey imagined, but reminded himself it was none of his business.

Lund hung over the rail, smoking, or paced the deck, always close to Rainey. The manner in which he went about the ship was almost uncanny. Except that his arms were generally ahead of him when he moved, his hands, with their woolly covering of red hair, lightly touching boom or rope or rail, he showed no hesitation, made no mistakes.

He no longer shuffled, as he had on shore, but moved with a pantherlike dexterity, here and there at will. When the breeze was steady he would even take the wheel and steer perfectly by the "feel of the wind" on his cheek, the slap of it in the canvas, or the creak of the rigging to tell him if he was holding to the course. And he took an almost childish delight in proclaiming his prowess as helmsman.

The booms were stayed out against swinging in flaws and the roll of the sea, and Lund strode back and forth behind Rainey, who had the wheel. The hunters were grouped about Carlsen, who, seated on the skylight, was telling them something at which they guffawed at frequent intervals.

"Spinnin' them some of his smutty yarns," growled Lund, halting in his promenade. "Bad for discipline, an' bad for us. He's the sort of fine-feathered bird that wouldn't give those chaps a first look ashore. Gittin' in solid with 'em that way is a bad steer. You can't handle a man you make a pal of, w'en he ain't yore rank."

"Carlsen's slack, but he's a good sailorman," said Rainey casually.

"Damn' sight better sailorman than he is doctor," retorted Lund. "Hear him the other mornin' w'en I asked him if he c'ud give me somethin' to help my eyes hurtin'? 'I'm no eye specialist,' sez he. 'Try some boracic acid, my man.' I wouldn't put ennything in my eyes *he'd* give me, you can lay to that. He'd give me vitriol, if he thought I'd use it. I wouldn't let him treat a sick cat o' mine. He's the kind o' doctor that uses his title to give him privileges with the wimmin. I know his sort."

Rainey wondered why Lund had asked Carlsen for a lotion if he did not mean to use it, but he did not provoke further argument. Lund was going on.

"He don't do the skipper enny good, thet's certain."

"Captain Simms seems to believe in him," answered Rainey. He wondered how much of Carlsen's increasing dominance over the skipper Lund had noticed.

"Simms is Carlsen's dog!" exploded Lund. "The doc's got somethin' on him, mark me. Carlsen's a bad egg an', w'en he hatches, you'll see a buzzard. An' you wait till he's needed as a doctor on somethin' that takes more'n a few kind words or a lick out a bottle."

There was a stir among the hunters. Lund turned his spectacled eyes in their direction.

"What are they up to now?" he queried. "Goin' to play poker? Wish I had my eyes. I'd show 'em how to read the pips."

Hansen came aft, offering to take the wheel.

"They bane goin' to shute at targets," he said. "Meester Carlsen he put up prizes. For rifle an' shotgun. Thought you might like to watch it, sir."

Rainey gave over the spokes and went to the starboard rail with Lund, watching the preparations between fore and main masts for the competition, and telling Lund what was happening. Carlsen gave out some shotgun cartridges from cardboard boxes, twelve to each of the six hunters.

"Hunters pay for their own shells," said Lund. "But they buy 'em from the ship. Mate's perkisite. They usually have some shells on hand for the rifles, but the paper cases o' the shotgun cartridges suck up the damp an' they keep better in the magazine in the cabin. What they shootin' at? Bottles?"

Sandy, the roustabout, had been requisitioned to toss up empty bottles, and those who failed cursed him for a poor thrower. A hunter named Deming made no misses, and secured first prize of ten dollars in gold, with a man named Beale scoring two behind him, and getting half that amount from Carlsen.

Then came the test with the rifles. The weapons were all of the same caliber, well oiled, and in perfect condition. As Lund had said, each of the hunters had a few shells in his possession, but they lacked the total of six dozen by a considerable margin.

Carlsen went below for the necessary ammunition while the target was completed and set in place. A keg had been rigged with a weight underslung to keep it upright, and a tin can, painted white, set on a short spar in one end of the keg. A light line was attached to a bridle, and the mark lowered over the stern, where it rode, bobbing in the tail of the schooner's wake, thirty fathoms from the taffrail where the crowd gathered.

Carlsen, returning, ordered Hansen to steer fine. He gave each competitor a limit of ten seconds for his aim, contributing an element of chance that made the contest a sporting one. Without the counting, each would have deliberately waited for the most favorable moment when the schooner hung in the trough and the white can was backed by green water. As it was, it made a far-from-easy mark, slithering, lurching, dipping as the *Karluk* slid down a wave or met a fresh one, the can often blurred against the blobs of foam.

More bullets hit the keg than the can, and Carlsen was often called upon as umpire. But the tin gradually became ragged and blotched where the steel-jacketed missiles tore through. Beale and Deming both had five clean, undisputed hits, tying for first prize. Beale offered to shoot it off with six more shells apiece, and Deming consented.

"Can't be done," declared Carlsen. "Not right now, anyway. I gave out the last shell there was in the magazine. If there are any more the skipper's got them stowed away, and I can't disturb him."

"Derned funny," said Deming, "a sealer shy on cartridges! Lucky we ain't worryin' about thet sort of a cargo."

"Probably plenty aboard somewhere," said Carlsen, "but I don't know where they are. Sorry to break up the shooting. You boys have got me beaten on rifles and shotguns," he went on, producing from his hip pocket a flat, effective-looking automatic pistol of heavy caliber. "How are you on small arms?"

The hunters shook their heads dubiously.

"Never use 'em," said Deming. "Never could do much with that kind, ennyhow. Give me a revolver, an' I might make out to hit a whale, if he was close enough, but not with one o' them."

"Not much difference," said, Carlsen. "Any of you got revolvers?"

No one spoke. It was against the unwritten laws of a vessel for pistols to be owned forward of the main cabin. Beale finally answered for the rest.

"Nary a pistol, sir."

"Then," said Carlsen, "I'll give you an exhibition myself. Any bottles left? Beale, will you toss them for me?"

There were eight shots in the automatic, and Carlsen smashed seven bottles in mid-air. He missed the last, but retrieved himself by breaking it as it dipped in the wake. The hunters shouted their appreciation.

"Break all of 'em?" Lund asked Rainey. "Enny bottles left at all?"

He walked toward the taffrail, addressing Carlsen.

"Kin you shoot by *sound* as well as by sight, Doc?" he challenged.

"I fancy not," said Carlsen.

"If I had my eyes I'd snapshoot ye for a hundred bucks," said Lund. "As it is, I might target one or two. Rainey, have some one run a line, head-high, an' fix a bottle on it, will ye? I ain't got a gun o' my own, Doc," he continued, "will you lend me yours?" Carlsen filled his clip and Lund turned toward Rainey, who was rigging the target.

"I'll want you to tap it with a stick," he said. "Signal-flag staff'll do fine."

Rainey got the slender bamboo and stood by. Lund felt for the cord, passed his fingers over the suspended bottle and stepped off five paces, hefting the automatic to judge its balance.

"Ruther have my own gun," he muttered. "All right, tetch her up, Rainey."

Rainey tapped the bottle on the neck and it gave out a little tinkle, lost immediately in the crash of splintering glass as the bottle, hit fairly in the torn label, broke in half.

"How much left?" asked Lund. "Half? Tetch it up."

Again he fired and again the bullet found the mark, leaving only the neck of the bottle still hanging. Lund grinned.

"Thet's all," he said. "Jest wanted to show ye what a blind man can do, if he's put to it."

There was little applause. Carlsen took his gun in silence and moved forward with the hunters and the onlookers, disappearing below. Rainey took the wheel over from Hansen and ordered him forward again.

"Given 'em something to talk about," chuckled Lund. "Carlsen wanted to show off his fancy shootin'. Wal, I've shown 'em I ain't entirely wrecked if I ain't carryin' lights. An' I slipped more'n one over on Carlsen at that."

Rainey did not catch his entire meaning and said nothing.

"Did you get wise to the play about the shells?" asked Lund. "A smart trick, though Deming almost tumbled. Carlsen got those dumb fools of hunters to fire away every shell they happened to have for'ard. If the magazine's empty, I'll bet Carlsen knows where they's plenty more shells, if we ever needed 'em bad. But now those rifles an' shotguns ain't no more use than so many clubs — *not to the hunters*. An' he's found out they ain't got enny pistols. *He's* got one, an' shows 'em how straight he shoots, jest in case there should be enny trubble between 'em. Plays both ends to the middle, does Carlsen. Slick! But he ain't won the pot. They's a joker in this game. Mebbe he holds it, mebbe not."

He nodded mysteriously, well pleased with himself.

"Don't suppose *you* brought a gun along with ye?" he asked Rainey. "Might come in handy."

"I wasn't expecting to stay," Rainey replied dryly, "or I might have."

Lund laughed heartily, slapping his leg.

"That's a good un," he declared. "It would have bin a good idea, though. It sure pays to go heeled when you travel with strangers."

CHAPTER IV
THE BOWHEAD

Captain Simms appeared again in the cabin and on deck, but he was not the same man. His illness seemed to have robbed him permanently of what was left him of the spring of manhood. It was as if his juices had been sucked from his veins and arteries and tissues, leaving him flabby, irresolute, compared to his former self. Even as Lund shadowed Rainey, so Simms shadowed Carlsen.

The fine weather vanished, snuffed out in an hour and, day after day, the *Karluk* flung herself at mocking seas that pounded her bows with blows that sounded like the noise of a giant's drum. The sun was never seen. Through daylight hours the schooner wrestled with the elements in a ghastly, purplish twilight, lifting under double reefs over great waves that raised spuming crests to overwhelm her, and were ridden down, hissing and roaring, burying one rail and covering the deck to the hatches with yeasty turmoil.

The *Karluk* charged the stubborn fury of the gale, rolling from side to side, lancing the seas, gaining a little headway, losing leeway, fighting, fighting, while every foot of timber, every fathom of rope, groaned and creaked perpetually, but endured.

To Rainey, this persistent struggle — as he himself controlled the schooner, legs far astride, his oilskins dripping, his feet awash to the ankles, spume drenching and whipping him, the wind a lash — brought exultation and a sense of mastery and confidence such as he had never before held suggestion of. To guide the ship, constantly to baffle the sea and wind, the turbulence, buffeting bows and run and counter, smashing at the rudder, leaping always like a pack of yapping hounds — this was a thing that left the days of his water-front detail far behind.

And then he had thought himself in the whirl of things! Even as Simms seemed to be declining, so Rainey felt that he was coming into the fulness of strength and health.

Lund was ever with him. Sometimes the girl would come up on deck in her own waterproofs and stand against the rail to watch the storm, silent as far as the pair were concerned. And presently Carlsen would come from below or forward and stand to talk with her until she was tired of the deck.

They did not seem much like lovers, Rainey fancied. They lacked the little intimacies that he, though he made himself somewhat of an automaton at the wheel, could not have failed to see. If the girl slipped, Carlsen's hand would catch and steady her by the arm; never go about her waist. And there was no especial look of welcome in her face when the doctor came to her.

Carlsen seldom took over the wheel. Rainey did more than his share from sheer love of feeling the control. But one day, at a word from the girl, Carlsen and she came up to Rainey as he handled the spokes.

"I'll take the wheel a while, Rainey," said the doctor.

Rainey gave it up and went amidships. Out of the tail of his eye he could see that the girl was pleading to handle the ship, and that Carlsen was going to let her do so.

Rainey shrugged his shoulders. It was Carlsen's risk. It was no child's play in that weather to steer properly. The *Karluk*, with her narrow beam, was lithe and active as a great cat in those waves. It took not only strength, but watchfulness and experience to hold the course in the welter of cross-seas.

Lund, whose recognition of voices was perfect, moved amidships as soon as Carlsen and Peggy Simms came aft. There was no attempt at disguising the fact that the schooner's afterward was a divided company and, save for the fact of his blindness tempering the action, the manner of Lund's showing them his back and deliberately walking off would have been a deliberate insult.

Not to the girl, Rainey thought. At first he had considered Lund's character as comparatively simple — and brutal — but he had qualified this, without seeming consciousness, and he felt that Lund would never deliberately insult a woman — any sort of woman. He was beginning to feel something more than an admiration for Lund's strength; a liking for the man himself had, almost against his will, begun to assert itself.

They stood together by the weather-rail. It was still Rainey's deck-watch, and at any moment Carlsen might relinquish the wheel back to him as soon as the girl got tired. Suddenly shouts sounded from forward, a medley of them, indistinct against the quartering wind. Sandy, the roustabout, came dashing aft along the sloping deck, catching clumsily at rail and rope to steady himself, flushed with excitement, almost hysterical with his news.

"A bowhead, sir!" he cried when he saw Rainey. "And killers after him! Blowin' dead ahead!"

Beyond the bows Rainey could see nothing of the whale, that must have sounded in fear of the killers, but he saw half a dozen scythe-like, black fins cutting the water in streaks of foam, all abreast, their high dorsals waving, wolves of the sea, hunting for the gray bowhead whale, to force its mouth open and feast on the delicacy of its living tongue. So Lund told him in swift sentences while they waited for the whale to broach.

"Ha'f the time the bowheads won't even try an' git away," said Lund. "Lie atop, belly up, plain jellied with fear while the killers help 'emselves. Ha'f the bowheads you git have got chunks bitten out of their tongues. If they're nigh shore when the killers show up the whales'll slide way out over the rocks an' strand 'emselves."

Rainey glanced aft. Sandy had carried his warning to Carlsen and the girl, and now was craning over the lee rail, knee-deep in the wash, trying to see something of the combat. Peggy Simms' lithe figure was leaning to one side as she, too, gazed ahead, though she still paid attention to her steering and held the schooner well up, her face bright with excitement, wet with flying brine, wisps of yellow hair streaming free in the wind from beneath the close grip of her woolen tam-o'-shanter bonnet of scarlet. Carlsen was pointing out the racing fins of the killers.

"Bl-o-ows!" started the deep voice of a lookout, from where sailors and hunters had grouped in the bows to witness this gladiatorial combat between sea monsters, staged fittingly in a sea that was running wild. Rainey strained his gaze to catch the steamy spiracle and the outthrust of the great head.

"Bl-o-ows!" The deep voice almost leaped an octave in a sudden shrill of apprehension. Other voices mingled with his in a clamor of dismay.

"Look out! Oh, look out! Dead ahead!"

The enormous bulk of the whale had appeared, not to spout, but to lie belly up, rocking on the surface with fins outspread, paralyzed with terror, directly in the course of the *Karluk*, while toward it, intent only on their blood lust, leaped the killers, thrusting at its head as the schooner surged down. In that tremendous sea the impact would be certain to mean the staving in of something forward, perhaps the springing of a butt.

"Hard a lee!" yelled Rainey. "Up with her! Up!"

It was desire to vent his own feelings, rather than necessity for the command, that made Rainey yell the order, for he could see the girl striving with the spokes, Carlsen lending his strength to hers. The sheets were well flattened, the wind almost abeam, and there was no need to change the set of fore and main.

Forward, the men jumped to handle the headsails. The *Karluk* started to spin about on its keel, instinct to the changing plane of the rudder. But the waves were running tremendously high, and the wind blowing with great force, the water rolling in great mountains of sickly greenish gray, topped with foam that blew in a level scud.

As the schooner hung in a deep trough, the wind struck at her, bows on. With the gale suddenly spilled out of them, the topsails lashed and shivered, and the fore broke loose with the sharp report of a gunshot and disappeared aft in the smother.

Rainey saw one huge billow rising, curving, high as the gaff of the main, it seemed to him, as he grasped at the coil of the main halyards. Down came the tons of water, booming on the deck that bent under the blow, spilling in a great cataract that swashed across the deck.

His feet were swept from under him, for a moment he seemed to swing horizontal in the stream, clutching at the halyards. The sea struck the opposite rail with a roar that threatened to tear it away, piling up and then seething overboard.

CHAPTER V
RAINEY SCORES

With it went a figure. Rainey caught sight of a ghastly face, a mouth that shouted vainly for help in the pandemonium, and was instantly stoppered with strangling brine, pop-eyes appealing in awful fright as Sandy was washed away in the cascade. The halyards were held on the pin with a turn and twist that Rainey swiftly loosened, lifting the coil free, making a fast loop, and thrusting head and arms through it as he flung himself after the roustabout.

Even as he dived he heard the bellow of Lund, knowing instinctively the peril of the schooner by its actions, though ignorant of the accident.

"Back that jib! Back it, blast yore eyes! Ba-ck — "

Then Rainey was clubbing his way through the race of water to where he glimpsed an upflung arm. Sandy was in oilskins and sea-boots, he had hardly a chance to save himself, however expert. And it flashed over Rainey's mind that, like many sailors, the lad had boasted that he could not swim. His boots would pull him under as soon as the force of the waves, that were tossing him from crest to crest, should be suspended. Rainey himself was borne on their thrust, clogged by his own equipment, linked to life only by the halyard coil.

A great bulk wallowed just before him, the helpless body of the bowhead whale, the killers darting in a mad mêlée for its head. Then a figure was literally hurled upon the slippery mass of the mammal, its gray belly plain in the welter, a living raft against which the waves broke and tossed their spray.

Clawing frantically, Sandy clutched at the base of the enormous pectoral fin, clinging with maniacal strength, mad with fear. Striking out to little purpose, save to help buoy himself, blinded by the flying scud and broken crests, Rainey felt himself upreared, swept impotently on and slammed against the slimy hulk, just close enough to Sandy to grasp him by the collar, as the whale, stung by a killer's tearing at its oily tongue, flailed with its fin and the two of them slid down its body, deep under water.

Rainey fought against the suffocation and the fierce desire to gasp and relieve his tortured lungs. The lad's weight seemed to be carrying him down as if he was a thing of lead, but Rainey would not relax his grip. He could not. He had centered all his energy upon the desire to save Sandy, and his nerve centers were still tense to that last conscious demand.

There came a swift, painful constriction of his chest that his failing senses interpreted only as the end of things. Then his head came out into the blessed air and he gulped what he could, though half of it was water.

The *Karluk* was into the wind and they were in what little lee there was, dragging aft at the end of the halyards, being fetched in toward the rail by the mighty tugs of Lund, a weird sight to Rainey's smarting eyes as he caught sight of the giant, with red hair uncovered, his beard whipping in the wind, his black glasses still in place, making some sort of a blessed monster out of him.

Rainey had his left fist welded to the line, his right was set in Sandy's collar, and Sandy's death clutch had twined itself into Rainey's oilskins, though the lad was limp, and his face, seen through the watery film that streamed over it, set and white.

A dozen arms shot down to grasp him. He felt the iron grip of Lund upon his left forearm, almost wrenching his arm from its socket as he was inhauled, caught at by body and legs and deposited on the deck of the schooner, that almost instantly commenced to go about upon its former course. Again he heard the bellow of the blind giant, as if it had been a continuation of the order shouted as he had gone overboard.

"Ba-ack that jib to win'ard! Ba-ck it, you swabs!"

The *Karluk* came about more smartly this time, swinging on the upheaval of a wave and rushing off with ever-increasing speed. Lund bent over him, asking him with a note that Rainey, for all his exhaustion, interpreted as one of real anxiety:

"How is it with you, matey? Did ye git lunged up?"

Rainey managed to shake his head and, with Lund's boughlike arm for support, got to his feet, winded, shaken, aching from his pounding and the crash against the whale.

"Good man!" cried Lund, thwacking him on the shoulder and holding him up as Rainey nearly collapsed under the friendly accolade.

Sandy was lying face down, one hunter kneeling across him, kneading his ribs to bellows action, lifting his upper body in time to the pressure, while another worked his slack arms up and down.

"I tank he's gone," said Hansen. "Swallowed a tubful."

"That was splendid, Mr. Rainey! Wonderful! It was brave of you!"

Peggy Simms stood before Rainey, clinging to the mainstays, a different girl to the one that he had known. Her red lips were apart, showing the clean shine of her teeth, above her glowing cheeks her gray eyes sparkled with friendly admiration, one slender wet hand was held out eagerly toward him.

"Why," said Rainey, in that embarrassment that comes when one knows he has done well, yet instinctively seeks to disclaim honors, "any one would have done that. I happened to be the only one to see it."

"I'm not so sure of that," replied the girl, and Rainey thought her lip curled contemptuously as she glanced toward Carlsen at the wheel. Yet Carlsen, he fancied, had full excuse for not having made the attempt, busied as he had been adding needed strength to the wheel.

"Oh, it was not what he did, or failed to do," said the girl, and this time there was no mistaking the fact that she emphasized her voice with contempt and made sure that it would carry to Carlsen. "He said it wasn't worth while."

Her eyes flashed and then she made a visible effort to control herself. "But it was very brave of you, and I want to ask your pardon," she concluded, with the crimson of her cheeks flooding all her face before she turned away, and made abruptly for the companion.

A little bewildered, the touch of her slim but strong fingers still sensible to his own, Rainey went to the wheel.

"Shall I take it over, Mr. Carlsen?" he asked. "It's my watch."

Carlsen surveyed him coolly. Either he pretended not to have heard the girl's innuendo or it failed to get under his skin.

"You'd better get into some dry togs, Rainey," he said. "And I'll prescribe a stiff jorum of grog-hot. Take your time about it." Rainey, conscious of a wrenched feeling in his side, a growing nausea and weakness, thanked him and took the advice. Half an hour later, save for a general soreness, he felt too vigorous to stay below, and went on deck again. Sandy had been taken forward. He encountered the hunter, Deming, and asked after the roustabout.

"Born to be hanged," answered the hunter with more friendliness than he had ever exhibited. "They pumped it out of him, and got his own pump to workin'. He'll be as fit as a fiddle presently. Asking for you."

"I'll see him soon," said Rainey, and again offered relief to Carlsen, which the doctor this time accepted.

"Miss Simms misunderstood me, Rainey," he said easily. "My intent was, that Sandy could never stay on top in those seas, and that it was idle to send a valuable man after a lout who was as good as dead. If it hadn't been for the whale you'd never have landed him. And the killers got the whale," he added, with his cynical grin.

So he had overheard. Rainey wondered whether the girl would accept the amended statement if it was offered. At its best interpretation it was callous.

When Hansen took over the watch Rainey went below to Sandy. Lund had disappeared, but he found the giant in the triangular forecastle by Sandy's bunk.

"That you, Rainey?" Lund asked as he heard the other's tread. Then he dropped his voice to a whisper:

"The lad's grateful. Make the most of it. If he wants to spill ennything, git all of it."

But Sandy seemed able to do nothing but grin sheepishly. He was half drunk with the steaming potion that had been forced down him.

"I'll see you later, Mister Rainey," he finally stammered out. "See you later, sir. You — I — "

Lund suddenly nudged Rainey in the ribs.

"Never mind now," he whispered.

A sailor had come into the forecastle with an extra blanket for Sandy, contributed from the hunters' mess.

"That's all right, Sandy," said Rainey. "Better try to get some sleep."

The roustabout had already dropped off. The seaman touched his temple in an old-fashioned salute.

"That was a smart job you did, sir," he said to Rainey.

The latter went aft with Lund through the hunters' quarters. They were seated under the swinging lamp which had been lit in the gloom of the gale, playing poker, as usual. But all laid down their cards as Rainey appeared.

"Good work, sir!" said one of them, and the rest chimed in with expressions that warmed Rainey's heart. He felt that he had won his way into their good-will. They were human, after all, he thought.

"Glad to have you drop in an' gam a bit with us, or take a hand in a game, sir," added Deming.

Rainey escaped, a trifle embarrassed, and passed through the alley that went by the cook's domain into the main cabin. Tamada was at work, but turned a gleam of slanting eyes toward Rainey as they passed the open door. The main cabin was empty.

"Come into my room," suggested Lund. "I want to talk with you."

He stuffed his pipe and proffered a drink before he spoke.

"Best day's work you've done in a long while, matey," he said quietly. "Take Deming's offer up, an' mix in with them hunters. An' pump thet kid, Sandy. Pump him dry. He'll know almost as much as Tamada, an' he'll come through with it easier."

"Just what are you afraid of?" asked Rainey.

"Son," said Lund simply, "I'm afraid of nothing. But they're primed for somethin', under Carlsen. We'll be makin' Unalaska ter-morrer or the next day. Here's hopin' it's the next. An' we've got to know what to expect. Did you know that the skipper has had another bad spell?"

"No. When?"

"Jest a few minnits ago. Cryin' for Carlsen like a kid for its nurse an' bottle. The doc's with him now. An' I'm beginnin' to have a hunch what's wrong with him. Here's somethin' for you to chew on: Inside of forty-eight hours there's goin' to be an upset aboard this hooker an' it's up to me an' you to see we come out on top. If not — "

He spread out his arms with the great, gorilla-like hands at the end of them, in a gesture that supplanted words. Beyond any doubt Lund expected trouble. And Rainey, for the first time, began to sense it as something approaching, sinister, almost tangible.

"You drop in on the hunters an' have a little game of poker ter-night," said Lund emphatically.

"I haven't got much money with me," said Rainey.

"Money, hell!" mocked Lund. "They don't play for money. They play for shares in the gold. They've got the big amount fixed at a million, each share worth ten thousand. 'Cordin' to the way things stand at present, you've got forty thousand dollars' worth in chips to gamble with. Put it up to 'em that way. I figger they'll accept it. If they don't, wal, we've learned something. An' don't forget to git next to Sandy."

A good deal of this was enigmatical to Rainey, but there was no mistaking Lund's tremendous seriousness and, duly impressed, Rainey promised to carry out his suggestions.

As he crossed the main cabin to go to his own room, Carlsen came out of the skipper's. He did not see Rainey at first and was humming a little air under his breath as he slipped a small article into his pocket. His face held a sneer. Then he saw Rainey, and it changed to a mask that revealed nothing. His tune stopped.

"I hear the captain's sick again," said Rainey. "Not serious, I hope."

Carlsen stood there gazing at him with his look of a sphinx, his eyes half-closed, the scoffing light showing faintly.

"Serious? I'm afraid it is serious this time, Rainey. Yes," he ended slowly. "I am inclined to think it is really serious." He turned away and rapped at the door of the girl's stateroom. In answer to a low reply he turned the handle and went in, leaving Rainey alone.

CHAPTER VI
SANDY SPEAKS

The next morning Rainey, going on deck to relieve Hansen at eight bells, in the commencement of the forenoon watch, found Lund in the bows as he walked forward, waiting for the bell to be struck. The giant leaned by the bowsprit, his spectacled eyes seeming to gaze ahead into the gray of the northern sky, and it seemed to Rainey as if he were smelling the wind. The sun shone brightly enough, but it lacked heat-power, and the sea had gone down, though it still ran high in great billows of dull green. There was a bite to the air, and Rainey, fresh from the warm cabin, wished he had brought up his sweater.

Lightly as he trod, the giant heard him and instantly recognized him.

"How'd ye make out with the hunters last night?" he queried. "I turned in early."

"We had quite a session," said Rainey. "They got me in the game, all right."

"Enny objections 'bout yore stakin' yore share in the gold?"

"Not a bit. I fancy they thought it a bit of a joke. More of one after we'd finished the game. I lost two thousand seven hundred dollars," he added with a laugh. "No chips under a dollar. Sky limit. And Deming had all the luck, and a majority of the skill, I fancy."

"Don't seem to worry you none."

"Well, it was sort of ghost money," laughed Rainey.

"You've seen the color of it," retorted Lund. "Hear ennything special?"

"No." Rainey spoke thoughtfully. "I had a notion I was being treated as an outsider, though they were friendly enough. But, somehow I fancy they reserved their usual line of talk."

"Shouldn't wonder," grunted Lund. "Seen Sandy yet?"

"I haven't had a chance. I imagined it would be best not to be seen talking to him."

"Right. Matey, things are comin' to a head. There's ice in the air. I can smell it. Feel the difference in temperature? Ice, all right. An' that means two things. We're nigh one of the Aleutians, an' Bering Strait is full of ice. Early, a bit, but there's nothin' reg'lar 'bout the way ice forms. I've got a strong hunch something'll break before we make the Strait."

"There's one thing in our favor. Yore savin' Sandy has set you solid with the hunters. They won't be so keen to maroon you. An' they'll think twice about puttin' me ashore blind. I used to git along fine with the hunters. All said an' done, they're men at bottom. Got their hearts gold-plated right now. But —"

He seemed obsessed with the idea that the crew, with Carlsen as prime instigator, had determined to leave them stranded on some volcanic, lonely barren islet. Rainey wondered what actual foundations he had for that theory.

"The sailors — " he started.

"Don't amount to a bunch of dried herrin'. A pore lot. Swing either way, like a patent gate. I ain't worryin' about them. I'm goin' to git my coffee. I was up afore dawn, tryin' to figger things out. You git to Sandy soon's you can, matey." And Lund went below.

Rainey saw nothing more of him until noon, at the midday meal. And he found no chance to talk with Sandy. He noticed the boy looking at him once or twice, wistfully, he thought, and yet furtively. A thickening atmosphere of something unusual afoot seemed present. And the actual weather grew distinctly colder. He had got his sweater, and he needed it. The sailors had put on their thickest clothes. Carlsen did not appear during the morning, neither did the hunters. Nor the girl.

At noon Carlsen came up to take his observation. He said nothing to Rainey, but the latter noticed the doctor's face seemed more sardonic than usual as he tucked his sextant under his arm.

With Hansen on deck they all assembled at the table with the exception of the captain. Tamada served perfectly and silently. The doctor conversed with the girl in a low voice. Once or twice she smiled across the table at Rainey in friendly fashion.

"Skipper enny better?" asked Lund, at the end of the meal.

Carlsen ignored him, but the girl answered:

"I am afraid not." It was not often she spoke to Lund at all, and Rainey wondered if she had experienced any change of feeling toward the giant as well as himself.

Carlsen got up, announcing his intention of going forward. Lund nodded significantly at Rainey as if to suggest that the doctor was going to foregather with the hunters, and that this might be an opportunity to talk with Sandy.

"Goin' to turn in," he said. "Eyes hurt me. It's the ice in the wind."

"Is there ice?" Peggy Simms asked Rainey as Lund disappeared. Carlsen had already vanished.

"None in sight," he answered. "But Lund says he can smell it, and I think I know what he means. It's cold on deck."

The girl went to the door of her own room and then hesitated and came back to the table where Rainey still sat. He had four hours off, and he meant to make an opportunity of talking to the roustabout.

"Mr. Carlsen told me he expects to sight land by to-morrow morning," she said. "Unalaska or Unimak, most likely. How is the boy you saved?"

She seemed so inclined to friendliness, her eyes were so frank, that Rainey resolved to talk to her. He held a notion that she was lonely, and worried about her father. There were pale blue shadows under her eyes, and he fancied her face looked drawn.

"May I ask you a question?" he asked.

"Surely."

"Just why did you beg my pardon? And, I may be wrong, but you seemed to make a point of doing so rather publicly."

She flushed slowly, but did not avoid his gaze, coming over to the table and standing across from him, her fingers resting lightly on the polished wood.

"It was because I thought I had misunderstood you," she said. "And I have thought it over since. I do not think that any man who would risk his life to save that lad could have joined the ship with such motives as you did. I — I hope I am not mistaken."

Rainey stared at her in astonishment.

"What motives?" he asked. "Surely you know I did not intend to go on this voyage of my own free will?"

The changing light in her eyes reminded Rainey of the look of her father's when he was at his best in some time of stress for the schooner. They were steady, and the pupils had dilated while the irises held the color of steel. There was something more than ordinary feminine softness to her, he decided. She sat down, challenging his gaze.

"Do you mean to tell me," she asked, "that you did not use your knowledge of this treasure to gain a share in it, under a covert threat of disclosing it to the newspaper you worked for?"

It was Rainey's turn to flush. His indignation flooded his eyes, and the girl's faltered a little. His wrath mastered his judgment. He did not intend to spare her feelings. What did she mean by such a charge? She must have known about the drugging. If not — she soon would.

"Your fiancé, Mr. Carlsen, told you that, I fancy," he said, "if you did not evolve it from your own imagination." Now her face fairly flamed.

"My fiancé?" she gasped. "Who told you that?"

"The gentleman himself," answered Rainey.

"Oh!" she cried, closing her eyes, her face paling.

"The same gentleman," went on Rainey vindictively, "who put chloral in my drink and deliberately shanghaied me aboard the *Karluk*, so that I only came to at sea, with no chance of return. He, too, was afraid I might give the snap away to my paper, though I would have given him my word not to. He told me it was a matter of business, that he had kidnapped me for my own good," he went on bitterly, recalling the talk with Carlsen when he had come out of the influence of the drug. "You don't have to believe me, of course," he broke off.

"I don't think you are quite fair, Mr. Rainey," the girl answered. "To me, I mean. I will give you *my* word that I knew nothing of this. I — " She suddenly widened her eyes and stared at him. "Then — my father — he?"

Rainey felt a twinge of compassion.

"He was there when it happened," he said. "But I don't know that he had anything to do with it. Mr. Carlsen may have convinced him it was the only thing to do. He seems to have considerable influence with your father."

"He has. He — Mr. Rainey, I have begged your pardon once; I do so again. Won't you accept it? Perhaps, later, we can talk this matter out. I am upset. But — you'll accept the apology, and believe me?"

She put out her hand across the table and Rainey gripped it.

"We'll be friends?" she asked. "I need a friend aboard the *Karluk*, Mr. Rainey."

He experienced a revulsion of feeling toward her. She was undoubtedly plucky, he thought; she would stand up to her guns, but she suddenly looked very tired, a pathetic figure that summoned his chivalry.

"Why, surely," he said.

They relinquished hands slowly, and again Rainey felt something more than her mere grasp lingering, a slight tingling that warmed him to smile at her in a manner that brought a little color back to her cheeks.

"Thank you," she said.

He watched her close the door of her cabin behind her before he remembered that she had not denied that she was to marry Carlsen. But he shrugged his shoulders as he started to smoke. At any rate, he told himself, she knows what kind of a chap he is — in what he calls business.

Presently he thought he heard her softly sobbing in her room, and he got up and paced the cabin, not entirely pleased with himself.

"I was a bit of a cad the way I went at her," he thought, "but that chap Carlsen sticks in my gorge. How any decent girl could think of mating up with him is beyond me — unless — by gad, I'll bet he's working through her father to pull it off! For the gold! If he's in love with her he's got a damned queer way of not showing it."

The door from the galley corridor opened, and a head was poked in cautiously. Then Sandy came into the cabin.

"Beg pardon, Mister Rainey, sir," said the roustabout, "I was through with the dishes. I wanted to have a talk with yer." His pop-eyes roamed about the cabin doubtfully.

"Come in here," said Rainey, and ushered Sandy into his own quarters.

"Now, then," he said, established on the bunk, while Sandy stood by the partition, slouching, irresolute, his slack jaw working as if he was chewing something, "what is it, my lad?"

"They'd kick the stuffin' out of me if they knew this," said Sandy. "I've bin warned to hold my tongue. Deming said he'd cut it out if I chattered. An' he would. But — "

"But what? Sit down, Sandy; I won't give you away."

"You went overboard after me, sir. None of them would. I've heard what Mr. Carlsen said, that I didn't ermount to nothin'. Mebbe I don't, but I've got my own reasons for hangin' on. Me, of course I don't ermount to much. Why would I? If I ever had mother an' father, I never laid eyes on 'em. I've made my own livin' sence I was eight. I've never 'ad enough grub in my belly till I worked for Tamada. The Jap slips me prime fillin'. He's only a Jap, but he's got more heart than the rest o' that bloody bunch put tergether."

Rainey nodded.

"Tell me what you know, quickly. You may be wanted any minute."

The words seemed to stick in the lad's dry throat, and then they came with a gush.

"It's the doc! It's Carlsen who's turned 'em into a lot of bloody bolsheviks, sir. Told 'em they ought to have an ekal share in the gold. Ekal all round, all except Tamada — an' me. I don't count. An' Tamada's a Jap. The men is sore at Mr. Lund becoz he sez the skipper left him be'ind on the ice. Carlsen's worked that up, too. Said Lund made 'em all out to be cowards.

'Cept Hansen, that is. He don't dare say too much, or they'd jump him, but Hansen sort of hints that Cap'n Simms ought to have gone back after Lund, could have gone back, is the way Hansen put it. So they're all goin' to strike."

Rainey's mind reacted swiftly to Sandy's talk. It seemed inconceivable that Carlsen would be willing to share alike with the hunters and the crew. Sandy's imagination had been running wild, or the men had been making a fool of him. The girl's share would be thrown into the common lot. And then flashed over him the trick by which Carlsen had disposed of all the ammunition in the hunters' possession. He had a deeper scheme than the one he fed to the hunters, and which he merely offered to serve some present purpose. Rainey's jaw muscles bunched.

"Go on, Sandy," he said tersely.

"There ain't much more, sir. They're goin' to put it up to Lund. First they figgered some on settin' him ashore with you an' the Jap. That's what Carlsen put up to 'em. But they warn't in favor of that. Said Lund found the gold, an' ought to have an ekal share with the rest. An' they're feelin' diff'runt about you, sir, since you saved me. Not becoz it was me, but becoz it was what Deming calls a damn plucky thing to do."

"How did you learn all this?" demanded Rainey.

"Scraps, sir. Here an' there. The sailors gams about it nights when they thinks I'm asleep in the fo'c's'le. An' I keeps my ears open when I waits on the hunters. But they ain't goin' to give you no share becoz you warn't in on the original deal. But they ain't goin' to maroon you, neither, unless Lund bucks an' you stand back of him."

"How about Captain Simms?"

"Carlsen sez he'll answer for him, sir. He boasts how he's goin' to marry the gal. That'll giv' him three shares — countin' the skipper's. The men don't see that, but I did. He's a bloody fox, is Carlsen."

"When's this coming off?" asked Rainey.

"Quick! They're goin' to sight land ter-morrer, they say. I heard that this mornin'. I hid in my bunk. It heads ag'inst the wall of the hunters' mess an', if it's quiet, you can hear what they say.

"They ain't goin' in to Bering Strait through Unimak Pass. They're goin' in through Amukat or Seguam Pass. An' they'll put it up to Lund an' the skipper somewheres close by there. An' that's where you two'll get put off, if you don't fall in line."

"All right, Sandy. You're smarter than I thought you were. Sure of all this?"

"I ain't much to look at, sir, but I ain't had to buck my own way without gittin' on ter myself. You won't give me away, though? They'd keelhaul me."

"I won't. You cut along. And if we happen to come out on top, Sandy, I'll see that you get a share out of it."

"Thank you, sir."

"I'll come out with you," said Rainey. "If any one comes in before you get clear, I'll give you an order. I sent for you, understand."

But Sandy got back into the galley without any trouble. Rainey began to pace the cabin again, and then went back into his own room to line the thing up. Lund was asleep, but he would waken him, he decided, filled with admiration at the blind man's sagacity and the way he had foreseen the general situation.

There was not much time to lose. He did not see what they could do against the proposition. He was sure that Lund would not consent to it. And he might have some plan. He had hinted that he had cards up his sleeve.

What Carlsen's ultimate plans were Rainey did not bother himself with. That it meant the fooling of the whole crew he did not doubt. He intended eventually to gather all the gold. And the girl — she would be in his power. But perhaps she wanted to be? Rainey got out of his blind alley of thought and started into the main cabin to give Lund the news.

The girl was coming out of her father's room.

"Any better?" asked Rainey.

"No. I can't understand it. He seems hardly to know me. Doctor Carlsen came along because of father's sciatica, but — there's something else — and the doctor can't help it any. I can't quite understand — "

She stopped abruptly.

"Have you known the doctor long?" asked Rainey.

"For a year. He lives in Mill Valley, close to my uncle. I live with my father's brother when father is at sea. But this time I wanted to be near him. And the doctor — "

Again she seemed to be deliberately checking herself from a revelation that wanted to come out.

"Did he practise in Mill Valley? Or San Francisco?" asked Rainey, remembering Lund's outburst against Carlsen's professional powers.

"No, he hasn't practised for some years. That was how it happened he was able to go along. Of course, father promised him a certain share in the venture. And he was a friend."

She trailed off in her speech, looking uncertainly at Rainey. The latter came to a decision.

"Miss Simms," he said, "are you going to marry Doctor Carlsen?"

Suddenly Rainey was aware that some one had come into the cabin. It was Carlsen, now swiftly advancing toward him, his face livid, his mouth snarling, and his black eyes devilish with mischief.

"I'll attend to this end of it," he said. "Peggy, you had better go in to your father. I'll be in there in a minute. He's a pretty sick man," he added.

His snarl had changed to a smile, and he seemed to have swiftly controlled himself. The girl looked at both of them and slowly went into the captain's room. Carlsen wheeled on Rainey, his face once more a mask of hate.

"I'll put you where you belong, you damned interloper," he said. "What in hell do you mean by asking her that question?"

"That is my business."

"I'll make it mine. And I'll settle yours very shortly, once and for all. I suppose you're soft on the girl yourself," he sneered. "Think yourself a hero! Do you think she'd look at you, a beggarly news-monger? Why, she — "

"You can leave her out of it," said Rainey, quietly. "As for you, I think you're a dirty blackguard."

Carlsen's hand shot back to his hip pocket as Rainey's fist flashed through the opening and caught him high on the jaw, sending him staggering back, crashing against the partition and down into the cushioned seat that ran around the place.

But his gun was out. As he raised it Rainey grappled with him. Carlsen pulled trigger, and the bullet smashed through the skylight above them, while Rainey forced up his arm, twisting it fiercely with both hands until the gun fell on the seat.

Simultaneously the girl and Lund appeared.

"Gun-play?" rumbled the giant. "That'll be you, Carlsen! You're too fond of shooting off that gat of yores."

Rainey had stepped back at the girl's exclamation. Carlsen recovered his gun and put it away, while Peggy Simms advanced with blazing eyes.

"You coward!" she said. "If I had thought — oh!"

She made a gesture of utter loathing, at which Carlsen sneered.

"I'll show you whether I'm a coward or not, my lady," he said, "before I get through with all of you. And I'll tell you one thing: The captain's life is in my hands. And he and I are the only navigators aboard this vessel, except a fool of a blind man," he added, as he strode to the door of Simms' cabin, turned to look at them, laughed deliberately in their faces, and shut the door on them.

CHAPTER VII
RAINEY MAKES DECISION

"Well?" asked Lund, "what are you goin' to do about it, Rainey? Stick with me, or line up with the rest of 'em, work yore passage, an' thank 'em for nothing when they divvy the stuff an' leave you out? You've got to decide one way or the other damn' quick, for the show-down's on the program for ter-morrer."

"You haven't said outright what you are going to do yourself," replied Rainey. "As for me, I seem to be between the devil and the deep sea. Carlsen has got some plan to outwit the men. It's inconceivable that he'll be willing to give them equal shares. And he has no use for me."

"You ought to have grabbed that gun of his before he did," said Lund. "He'll put you out of the way if he can, but, now his temper's b'iled over a bit, he'll not shoot you. Not afore the gold's in the hold. One thing, he knows the hunters wouldn't stand for it. They've got dust in their eyes right now — gold-dust, chucked there by Carlsen, but if he'd butchered you he'd likely lose his grip on 'em. I think he would. I don't believe yo're in enny danger, Rainey, if you want to buckle in an' line up with the crowd.

"As for me," he went on, his voice deepening, "I'm goin' to tell 'em to go plumb to hell. I'll tell Carlsen a few things first. Equal shares! A fine bunch of socialists they are! Settin' aside that Carlsen's bullin' 'em, as you say. Equal? They ain't my equal, none of 'em, man to man. All men are born free an' equal, says the Constitution an' by-laws of this country of ours. Granted. But they don't stay that way long. They're all lined up to toe the mark on the start, but watch 'em straggle afore they've run a tenth of the distance.

"I found this gold, an' they didn't. I don't have to divvy with 'em, an' I won't. A lot of I. W. W.'s, that's what they are, an' I'll tell 'em so. More'n that, if enny of 'em thinks he's my equal all he's got to do is say so, an' I'll give him a chance to prove it. Feel those arms, matey, size me up. Man to man, I c'ud break enny of 'em in half. Put me in a room with enny three of 'em, an' the door locked, an' one 'ud come out. That 'ud be me."

This was not bragging, not blustering, but calm assurance, and Rainey felt that Lund merely stated what he believed to be facts. And Rainey believed they were facts. There was a confident strength of spirit aside from his physical condition that emanated from Lund as steam comes from a kettle. It was the sort of strength that lies in a steady gale, a wind that one can lean against, an elastic power with big reserves of force. But the conditions were all against Lund, though he proceeded to put them aside.

"Man to man," he repeated, "I c'ud beat 'em into Hamburg steak. An' I've got brains enough to fool Carlsen. I've outguessed him so far."

"He's got the gun," warned Rainey.

"Never mind his gun. I ain't afraid of his gun." He nodded with such supreme confidence that Rainey felt himself suddenly relegating the doctor's possession of the gun to the background. "If his gun's the only thing trubblin' you, forget it. You an' me got to know where we stand. It's up to you. I won't blame you for shiftin' over. An' I can git along without you, if need be. But we've got along together fine; I've took a notion to you. I'd like to see you get a whack of that gold, an' all the devils in hell an' out of it ain't goin' to stop me from gittin' it!"

He talked in a low voice, but it rumbled like the distant roar of a bull. Rainey looked at the indomitable jaw that the beard could not hide, at the great barrel of his chest, the boughlike arms, the swelling thighs and calves, and responded to the suggestion that Lund could rise in Berserker rage and sweep aside all opposition.

It was absurd, of course; his next thought adjusted the balance that had been weighed down by the compelling quality of the man's vigor but, for the moment, remembering his earlier simile, Lund appeared a blind Samson who, by some miracle, could at the last moment destroy his enemies by pulling down their house — or their ship — about them.

"Carlsen says that the skipper's life is in his hands," he said, still evading Lund's direct question. "What do you make of that?"

"I don't know what to make of it," answered Lund. "If it is, God help the skipper! I reckon he's in a bad way. Ennyhow, he's out of it for the time bein', Rainey. I don't think he'll be present at the meetin' if he's that ill. Carlsen speaks for him. Count Simms out of it for the present."

"There's the girl," said Rainey. "I don't believe she wants to marry Carlsen."

"If she does," said Lund, "she ain't the kind we need worry about. Carlsen 'ud marry her if he thought it was necessary to git her share by bein' legal. He may try an' squeeze her to a wedding through the skipper. Threaten to let her dad die if she don't marry him, likely'll git the skipper to tie the knot. It 'ud be legal. But if you're interested about the gal, Rainey, an' I take it you are, I'm tellin' you that Carlsen'll marry her if it suits his book. If it don't, he won't. An', if he wins out, he'll take her without botherin' about prayer-books an' ceremonies. I know his breed. All men are more or less selfish an' shy on morals, in streaks more or less wide, but that Carlsen's just plain skunk."

"The men wouldn't permit that," said Rainey tersely. "If Carlsen started anything like that I'd kill him with my own hands, gun or no gun. And any white man would help me do it."

"You would, mebbe," said Lund, nodding sagely. "You'd have a try at it. But you don't know men, matey, not like I do. This ship's got a skipper now. A sick one, I grant you. But so far he's boss. An' he's the gal's father. All's usual an' reg'lar. But you turn this schooner into a free-an'-easy, equal shares-to-all, go-as-you-please outfit, let 'em git their claws on the gold, an' be on the way home to spend it — for Carlsen'll let 'em go that far afore he pulls his play, whatever it is — an' discipline will go by the board.

"Grog'll be served when they feel like it, they'll start gamblin', some of 'em'll lose all they got. There'll be sore-heads, an' they'll remember there's a gal in the after-cabin, which won't be the after-cabin enny more, for they'll all have the run of it, bein' equal; then all hell's goin' to break loose, far's that gal's concerned.

"A bunch of men who've bin at sea for weeks, half drunk, crazy over havin' more gold than they ever dreamed of, or havin' gambled it away. Jest a bunch of beasts, matey, whenever they think of that gal. They'll be too much for Carlsen to handle — an'" — he tapped at Rainey's knee — "Carlsen don't think enough of enny woman to let her interfere with his best interests."

Rainey's jaw was set and his fists clenched, his blood running hot and fast. His imagination was instinct to conjure up full-colored scenes from Lund's suggestions.

"You mean — " he began.

"Under his hide, when there ain't nothin' to hinder him, a man's plain animal," said Lund. "What do these water-front bullies know about a good gal — or care? They only know one sort. Ever think what happened to a woman in privateer days when they got one aboard, alone, on the high seas? Why, if they pushed Carlsen, he'd turn her over to 'em without winkin'."

"You hinted I was different," said Rainey. "How about you, Lund, how would you act?"

"If Carlsen wins out, I'd be chewin' mussels on a rock, or feedin' crabs," said Lund simply. "I'm no saint, but, so long as I can keep wigglin', there ain't enny hunter or seaman goin' to harm a decent gal. That's another way they ain't my equal, Rainey. Savvy? Nor is Carlsen. There ain't enough real manhood in that Carlsen to grease a skillet. How about it, Rainey; are you lined up with me?"

"Just as far as I can go, Lund. I'm with you to the limit."

Lund brought down his hand with a mighty swing, and caught at Rainey's in mid-air, gripping it till Rainey bit his lips to repress a cry of pain.

"You've got the guts!" cried the giant, checking the loudness of his voice abruptly. "I knew it. It ain't all goin' to go as they like it. Watch my smoke. Now, then, keep out of Carlsen's way all you can. He may try an' pick a row with you that'll put you in wrong all around. Go easy an' speak easy till land's sighted. If you ain't invited to this I. W. W. convention, horn in.

"Carlsen'll try an' keep you on deck, I fancy. Don't stay there. Turn the wheel over to Sandy if you have to. I'll insist on havin' you there. That'll be better. They'll probably have some fool agreement to sign. Carlsen would do that. Make 'em all feel it's more like a bizness meetin'.

They'll love to scrawl their names an' put down their marks. I'll have to have you there to read it over to me; savvy?"

"What do you think Carlsen's game is, if it goes through?"

"He's fox enough to think up a dozen ways. Run the schooner ashore somewhere in the night. Wreck her. Git 'em in the boats with the gold. Inside of a week, Deming an' one or two others would have won it all. Then — he'd have the only gun — he'd shoot the lot of 'em an' say they died at sea. He ain't got enny more warm blood than a squid. Or he might land, and accuse 'em all of piracy. What do we care about his plans? He ain't goin' to put 'em over."

Rainey had to relieve Hansen. He left Lund primed for resistance against Carlsen, against all the crew, if necessary, resolved to save the girl, but, as Lund stayed below and the time slid by, his confidence oozed out of him, and the odds assumed their mathematical proportion.

What could they do against so many? But he held firm in his determination to do what he could, to go down with the forlorn hope, fighting. Blind as he was, Lund was the better man of the two of them, Rainey felt; it was better to attempt to seize the horns of the dilemma than weakly to give way and, with Lund killed, or marooned, try single-handed to protect Peggy Simms against the horrors that would come later.

He did not believe himself in love with her. The environment had not been conducive to that sort of thing. But the thought of her, their hands clasped, her eyes appealing, saying she needed a friend aboard the *Karluk*; the young clean beauty of her, nerved him to stand with Lund against the odds. Lund was fighting for his rights, for his gold, but he had said that he would not see a decent girl harmed as long as he could wiggle. Rough sea-bully as the giant was, he had his code. Rainey tingled with contempt of his own hesitancy.

The *Karluk* was bowling along northward toward landfall and the crisis between Lund and Carlsen at good speed. The weather had subsided and the half gale now served the schooner instead of hindering her. Rainey turned over the wheel to a seaman and paced the deck. The bite in the air had increased until even the smart walk he maintained failed to circulate the blood sufficiently to keep his fingers from becoming benumbed, so that he had to beat his arms across his chest.

It was well below the freezing point. If they had been sailing on fresh water, instead of salt, he fancied that the rigging would have been glazed where the spray struck it. As it was, the canvas seemed to him stiffer than usual, and there was a whitish haze about the northern horizon that suggested ice.

The tall, olive-tinted seas ranged up in dissolving hills, the wind's whistle was shrill in the rigging. Over the mainmast a gray-breasted bird with wide, unmoving pinions hung without apparent motion, its ruby eyes watching the ship, as if it was a spy sent out from the Arctic to report the adventurous strangers about to dare its dangers.

As the day passed to sunset the gloom quickly deepened. The sun sank early into banks of leaden clouds, and the *Karluk* slid on through the seething seas in a scene of strange loneliness, save for the suspended albatross that never varied its position by an inch or by a flirt of its plumes.

Rainey felt the dreary suggestion of it all as he walked up and down, trying to evolve some plan. Lund's mysterious hints were unsatisfactory. He could not believe them without some basis, but the giant would never go further than vague talk of a "joker" or a card up his sleeve. And they would need more than one card, Rainey thought.

He wondered whether they could win over Hansen, who had spoken for Lund against the skipper. And had then kept his counsel. But he dismissed Hansen as an ally. The Scandinavian was too cautious, too apt to consider such things as odds. Sandy was useless, aside from his good-will. He was cowed by Deming, scared of Carlsen, too puny to do more than he had done, given them warning.

Tamada? Would he fight for the share of gold he expected to come to him? Lund had described him as neutral. But, if he knew that he was to be left out of the division? It was not likely that he would be called to the conference. The Japanese undoubtedly knew the racial prejudice against him, a prejudice that Rainey considered short-sighted, taking some pains to show that he did not share it. At any rate, Tamada might provide him with a weapon, a sharp-bladed vegetable knife if nothing better.

But, if it came to downright combat, they must be overwhelmed. Carlsen's gun again assumed proper proportions. Lund might not be afraid of it, but Rainey was, very frankly. He should have snatched it from the cabin cushions. But Tamada? He could not dismiss Tamada as an important factor. There was no question to Rainey but that Tamada was, by caste, above his position as sealer's cook. It was true that a Japanese considered no means menial if they led to the proper end.

Was that end merely to gain possession of his share of the gold, or did Tamada have some deeper, more complicated reason for signing on to run the galley of the *Karluk*? Somehow Rainey thought there was such a reason. He treated Tamada with a courtesy that he had found other Japanese appreciated, and fancied that Tamada gradually came to regard him with a certain amount of good-will. But it was hard to determine anything that went on back of those unfathomable eyes, or to read Tamada's face, smooth and placid as that of an ivory image.

CHAPTER VIII
TAMADA TALKS

Tamada's galley was as orderly and efficient as the operating-room of a first-class hospital. And Tamada at his work had all the deftness and some of the dignity of a surgeon. There was no wasted move, there was no litter of preparation, every article was returned to its specified place as soon as used, and every implement and utensil was shining and spotless.

It was an hour from the third meal of the day. Tamada was juggling the food for three messes, and he was doing it with the calm precision of one who has every detail well mapped out and is moving on schedule. The boy Sandy was not there, probably engaged in laying the table for the hunters' mess, Rainey imagined.

Tamada regarded him with eyes that did not lack a certain luster, as a sloeberry might hold it, but which, beneath their hooded lids, revealed neither interest, nor curiosity, nor friendliness. They belonged in his unwrinkled face, they were altogether neutral. Yet they seemed covertly to suggest to Rainey that they might, on occasion, flame with wrath or hatred, or show the burning light of high intelligence. Seldom, he thought, while their gaze rested on him impassively, would they soften.

"Tamada," he queried, "you think I am your friend, that I would rather help you than otherwise?"

"I think that — yes?" answered the Japanese without hesitation and without servility. And his eyes slowly searched Rainey's face with appraising pertinacity for a second or two. His English, save for the oddness of his idioms and a burr that made *r's* of most his *l's*, and sometimes reversed the process, was almost perfect. His vocabulary showed study. "You are not hating me because you are Californian and I Japanese," he said. "I know that."

There was little time to spare, and there was likelihood of interruption, so Rainey plunged into his subject without introduction.

"They promised you a share of this treasure, Tamada?" he asked.

"They promised me that, yes."

"They do not intend to give it to you." There was a tiny, dancing flicker in the dark eyes that died like a spark in the night air. Rainey recalled Lund's opinion that little went on that Tamada did not know. "You may have guessed this," he hurried on, "but I am sure of it. I, too, am promised some of the gold, but they do not intend to give it to me. They will offer Mr. Lund only a small portion of what was originally arranged, the same amount as the rest of them are to get. He will refuse that to-morrow, when a meeting is to be called. Then there will be trouble. I shall stand with Mr. Lund. If we win you will get your share, whether you help us or not. If you help us I can promise you at least twice the amount you were to get."

"How can I help you? If this is to be talked over at a meeting I shall not be allowed to be present. If trouble starts it will do so immediately. Mr. Lund" — he called it Rund — "is not patient man. What can I do? How can I help you?"

Rainey was nonplused. He had seized the first opportunity of sounding the Japanese, and he had nothing outlined.

"I do not know," he said. "I must talk that over with Mr. Lund. I wanted to know if you would be on our side."

"Mr. Lund will not want me to help you. He does not like color of my skin, he does not like Japanese because he thinks they make too good living in California, and making more money than some of his countrymen. I do not think it help you for me to join. I do not see how you can win. If you can show some way out I will do what I can. But I like to see way out."

He mollified the bald acknowledgment of his neutrality with a little bow and a hissing-in breath. Back of it all was a will that was inflexible, thought Rainey.

"If we lose, you lose," he went on lamely. He had come on a fool's errand, he decided.

"I think I shall get my money," said Tamada, and something looked out of his eyes that betrayed a purpose already gained, Rainey fancied, as a chess player might gain assurance of victory by the looking ahead to all conceivable moves against him, and providing a counter-play that would achieve the game. It was borne in upon him that Tamada had resources he could not fathom. The Oriental gave a swift smile, that held no mirth, no friendship, rather, a sardonic appreciation of the situation, without rancor.

"They are very foolish," he said. "They make me cook, they eat what I serve. They say Tamada is very good cook. But he is Jap, damn him. Suppose I put something in that food, that they would not taste? I could send them all to sleep. I could kill them. I could do it so they never suspect, but would go to their beds — and never get up from them. It would be very easy. Yet they trust me."

The statement was so matter-of-fact that Rainey felt his horror gather slowly as he stared at the impassive Oriental.

"You would do that? What good would it do you? You would have to kill them all, or the rest would tear you apart. And if you murdered the whole ship where would you be? You talk as if you were a little mad. Suppose I told Carlsen of this?"

Tamada was smiling again. He seemed to know that Rainey was in no position to betray him — if he wished to do so.

"I did not say I would do it. And, except under certain circumstances, it do me little good. I do not expect to do it. But it would be easy. Yet, as you say, it would not help you to kill only few, those who will be at the meeting, for example, even if I wish to do. No, I do not see way out. If, at any time there should seem way out and I can help you, I will."

He turned abruptly to a simmering pot and rattled the lid. The hunter, Deming, stuck his head in at the door.

"Smells good," he said. "Evening, Mr. Rainey."

He seemed disposed to linger, and Rainey, not to excite suspicion toward himself or Tamada, went back on deck. What did Tamada mean by "except under certain circumstances"? he asked himself. For one thing he felt sure that Tamada had some basis for his expression that he expected to get his money. *He knew something.* Was it merely the Oriental method of *jiu-jitsu*, practised mentally as well as physically, the belief in a seemingly passive resistance against circumstances, waiting for some move that, by its own aggressiveness, would give him an opening for a trick that would secure him the advantage? What could one Japanese hope to do against the crowd?

A thought suddenly flashed over Rainey. Was Tamada in league with Carlsen? Had he mistaken his man? Did Carlsen plan to have Tamada undertake a wholesale poisoning to secure the gold himself, providing the drugs? Was it a friendly hint from the Japanese?

Still mulling over it he went down to supper. The girl was not present. Carlsen appeared in an unusual mood.

"I was a bit hasty, Rainey," he said, with all appearance of sincerity. "I've been worried a bit over the skipper. He's in a bad way.

"Forget what happened, if you can. I apologize. Though I still think your interference in my private affairs unwarranted. I'll call it square, if you will."

He nodded across the table at Rainey, saving the latter a reply which he was rather at a loss how to word. Amenities from Carlsen were likely a Greek gift. And Carlsen rattled on during the meal in high good spirits, rallying Rainey about his poker game with the hunters, joking Lund about his shooting, talking of the landfall they expected the next day.

To Rainey's surprise Lund picked up the talk. There was a subtle, sardonic flavor to it on both sides and, once in a while, as Tamada, like an animated sphinx, went about his duties, Rainey saw the eyes of Carlsen turned questioningly upon the giant as if a bit puzzled concerning the exact spirit of his sallies.

Rainey admired while he marveled at the sheer skill of Lund in this sort of a fencing bout. He never went far enough to arouse Carlsen's suspicions, yet he showed a keen sense of humorous appreciation of Carlsen's half-satirical sallies that, in the light of Sandy's revelation, showed the doctor considered himself the master of the situation, the winner of a game whose pieces were already on the board, though the players had not yet taken their places. Yet Rainey fancied that Carlsen qualified his dismissal of Lund as a "blind fool" before they rose from the table, without disturbing his own equanimity as the craftier of the two.

Later, when his watch was ended and he was closeted with Lund in the latter's cabin, the giant promptly quashed all discussion of Tamada's attitude.

"I'll put no trust in any slant-eyed, yellow-skinned rice-eater," he announced emphatically. "They're against us, race an' religion. They want California, or rather, the Pacific coast, an' they think they're goin' to git it. They're no more akin to us than a snake is a cousin to an eel. They're not of our breed, an' you can't mix the two. I'll have no deal with Tamada, beyond gettin' dope out of him. If he helped us it 'ud be only to further his own ends. Not that he can do much — unless — "

He lowered his voice to a husky whisper.

"There's one thing may slip in our gold-gettin', matey," he said — "the Japanese. I doubt if this island is set down on American or British charts. But I'll bet it is on the Japanese. I don't know as any nation has openly claimed it, but it's a sure thing the Japs know of its existence. They don't know of the gold, or it wouldn't be there. Rightly, the island may belong to Russia, but, since the war, Russia's in a bad way, an' ennything loose from the mainland'll be gobbled by Japan.

"What the Japs grab they don't let go of. On general principles they patrol the west side of Bering Strait. If one of their patrols sees us we'll be inside the sealin' limit, an' they'll have right of search. They'd take it, ennyway, if they sighted us. They go by *power* of search, not right. They won't find enny pelts on us, we've got hunters aboard, we're pelagic sealers, they won't be able to hang up enny clubbin' of herds on us.

"But, if they should suspicion us of gittin' gold off enny island they c'ud trump up to call theirs, if they found gold on us at all, it 'ud be all off with us an' the *Karluk*. We'd be dumped inside of some Jap prison an' the schooner confiscated.

"An', if things go right with us, an' we ever sight the smoke of a Jap gunboat comin' our way, the first thing I'll be apt to do will be to scrag Tamada or he'll blow the whole proposition, whether we've got the gold aboard or not. Even if he didn't want to tell becoz of his own share, they'd git it out of him what we was after."

Did this, wondered Rainey, explain Tamada's "certain circumstances"? Was he calculating on the arrival of a Japanese patrol? Had he already tipped off to his consul in San Francisco the purpose of the expedition, sure of a reward equal to what his share would have been? If so, Rainey had made a muddle of his attempt to sound Tamada. He felt guilty, glad that Lund could not see his face, and he dropped the subject abruptly.

Lund seemed to know that something was amiss.

"Nervous, Rainey?" he asked. "That's becoz you've not bin livin' a man's life. All yore experience has bin second-hand, an' you've never gone into a rough-an'-tumble, I take it. You'll make out all right if it comes to that at all. Yo're well put up, an' you've got solid of late. Now yo're goin' to git a taste of life in the raw. Not story-book stuff. It's strong meat sometimes, an' liable to turn some people's stomachs. I've got an appetite for it, an' so'll you have, after a bit.

"Ever play much at cards?" he went on. "Play for yore last red when you don't know where to turn for another, an' have all the crowd thinkin' yo're goin' broke as they watch the play? An' then you slap down a card they've all overlooked an' larf in the other chap's face?

"That's what I'm goin' to do with Carlsen. I've got that kind of a card, matey, an' I ain't goin' to spoil my fun by tellin' even you what it is, though yo're my partner in this gamble. It's a trump, an' Carlsen's overlooked it. He figgers he's stacked the deck an' fixed it so's he deals himself all the winnin' cards. But there's one he don't know is there becoz he's more of a blind fool than I am, is Doctor Carlsen."

Lund chuckled hugely as he mixed himself some whisky and water. Rainey refused a drink. Lund was right, he was nervous, bothering over what the outcome might be, and how he might handle himself. He was not at all sure of his own grit.

Lund had hit the nail on the head. All his experience had lain in listening to the stories of others and writing them down. He did not know whether he would act in a manner that would satisfy himself. There was a nasty doubt as to his own prowess and his own courage that kept cropping up. And that state of mind is not a pleasant one.

"All be over this time ter-morrer," put in Lund, "so far as our bisness with Carlsen is concerned. You git all the sleep you can ter-night, Rainey. An' don't you worry none about that gal. She's a damn' sight more capable of lookin' after herself than you imagine. You ain't counted her in as bein' more than a clingin' vine proposition. Not that she could buck it on her own, but she's no fool, an' I bet she's game.

"Soft on her?" he challenged unexpectedly.

"I haven't thought of her in that way," Rainey answered, a bit shortly.

"Ah!" the giant ejaculated softly. "You haven't? Wal, mebbe it's jest as well."

Rainey took that last remark up on deck and pondered over it in the middle watch, but he could make nothing out of it. Yet he was sure that Lund had meant something by it.

In the middle of the night the cold seemed to concentrate. Rainey had found mittens in the schooner's slop-chest, and he was glad of them at the wheel. The sailors, with but little to do, huddled forward. One man acted as lookout for ice. The smell of this was now unmistakable even to Rainey's inexperience. On certain slants of wind a sharper edge would come that bit through ordinary clothes. It was, he thought, as if some one had suddenly opened in the dark the doors of an enormous refrigerator. He knew what that felt like, and this was much the same.

The weather was still clearing. In the sky of indigo the stars were glittering points, not of gold, but steel, hard and cold. Ahead, the northern lights were projected above the horizon in a low arch of quivering rose. And, out of the north, before the wind, the sea advanced in the long, smooth folds of a weighty swell over which the *Karluk* wore her way into the breeze, clawing steadily on to the Aleutians and a passage through to Bering Strait.

At two bells the hunters began to come on deck for a breath or so of fresh air after the closeness of their quarters, as they invariably did following a poker session. They did not come aft or give any greeting to Rainey, but walked briskly about in couples, discussing something that Rainey did not doubt was the next day's meeting. Doubtless, in the confidence of their numbers, they considered it a mere formality. Lund would take what they offered — or nothing. And Carlsen had guaranteed the skipper's signature to an agreement.

They got their lungs recharged with good air, and then the cold drove them below, and Rainey, with the length of the schooner between him and the watch, was practically alone. He went over and over the situation as a squirrel might race around the bars of his revolving cylinder, and came to only one conclusion, the inevitable one, to let the matter develop itself. Lund's winning card he had bothered about until his brain was tired. The only thing he got out of all his fussing was the one new thought that seemed to fly out at a tangent and mock him.

If Carlsen was deposed, and the skipper continued ill — to face the worst but still plausible — if Carlsen, being deposed, refused to act, and the skipper was too sick to leave his room — who was going to navigate the schooner? Not a blind man. And Rainey couldn't learn navigation in a day. There was more to it in these perilous seas than mere reckoning. Ice was ahead.

What could Lund make of that? Supposing that card of his did win, how could they handle the schooner? He, in his capacity of eyes for Lund, would be about as competent as a poodle trying to lead a blind pedler out of a maze.

The lookout broke in on his mulling over with a sudden shout.

"*Ice! Ice!* Close on the starboard bow!"

Rainey put the helm over, throwing the *Karluk* on the opposite tack.

The berg slipped by them, not as he had imagined it, a thing of sparkling minarets and pinnacles, but a hill of snow that materialized in the soft darkness and floated off again to dissolution like the ghost of an island, leaving behind the bitter chill of death, rising and falling until, in a moment, it was gone, with its threat of shipwreck had the night been less clear.

Five times before eight bells the cry came from forward, and the heaps of shining whiteness would take form, gather a certain sharpness of outline, and go past the beam with the seas surging about them and breaking with a hollow boom upon their cavernous sides. And this was in the open sea. Lund had suggested that the strait would be full of ice. Rainey felt his sailing experience, that he came to be rather proud of, pitifully limited and inadequate in the face of coming conditions.

When he turned in at last, despite his determination to follow Lund's admonition concerning sleep, it would not come to him. Hansen had taken over the deck stolidly enough, with no show of misgivings as to his ability to handle things, but his words had not been cheering to Rainey.

"Plenty ice from now on, Mr. Rainey. Now we bane goin' to have one hard yob on our hands, by yiminy, you an' me!"

CHAPTER IX
THE POT SIMMERS

Rainey was awakened at half past seven by the swift rush of men on deck and a confused shouting. The sun was shining brightly through his porthole and then it became suddenly obscured. He looked out and saw a turreted mass of ice not half a cable's length away from the schooner, water cascading all over its hills and valleys, that were distinct enough, but so smoothed that the truth flashed over him. Here was a berg that had suddenly turned turtle and exposed its greater, under-water bulk to the air.

About it the sea was dark and vivid blue, and the berg sparkled in the sun with prismatic reflections that gave all the hues of the rainbow to its prominences, while the bulk glowed like a fire opal. Between it and the schooner the sea ran in a lasher of diminishing turmoil. Hansen had carelessly sailed too close. The momentum of the *Karluk* and its slight wave disturbance must have sufficed to upset the equilibrium of the berg, floating with only a third of its bulk above the water. And the displacement had narrowly missed the schooner's side.

He got a cup of coffee after dressing warmly, and went up. Carlsen and the girl had preceded him and were gazing at the iceberg. The doctor seemed to be in the same rare vein of humor as overnight. Lund stood at the rail with his beak of a nose wrinkled, snuffing toward the icy crags that were spouting a dazzle of white flame, set about with smaller, sudden flares of ruby, emerald and sapphire.

"Close shave, that, Rainey," called Carlsen. "She turned turtle on us."

"Too close to be pleasant," said Rainey, and went to the wheel. The girl had given him a smile, but he marked her face as weary from sleeplessness and strain. Rainey left the spokes in charge of Hansen for a minute — Hansen stolid and chewing like an automaton, undisturbed by the incident now it had passed — and asked the girl how her father was.

"I am afraid — " she began, then glanced at Carlsen.

"He is not at all well," said the doctor, facing Rainey, his face away from the girl. As he spoke he left his mouth open for a moment, his tongue showing between his white teeth, in a grin that was as mocking as that of a wolf, mirthless, ruthless, triumphant. And for a fleeting second his eyes matched it.

Rainey restrained a sudden desire to smash his fist into that sardonic mask. This was the day of Carlsen's anticipated victory, the first of his calculated moves toward check-mate, and he was palpably enjoying it.

"Not — at — all — well," repeated Carlsen slowly. "He needs something to bring him out of himself, as he now is. A little excitement. Yet he should not be crossed in any way. We shall see."

He shifted his position and looked at the girl much as a wolf, not particularly hungry, might look at a tethered lamb. His tongue just touched the inner edges of his lips. It was as if the wolf had licked his chops.

"Carlsen would be a bad loser," Lund had once said, "and a nasty winner. He'd want to rub it in as soon as he knew he had you beat."

Rainey gripped the spokes hard until he felt the pressure of his bones against the wood. Carlsen's attitude had had one good effect. His nervousness had disappeared, and a cold rage taken its place. He could cheerfully have attempted to throttle Carlsen without fear of his gun. For that matter, he had faced the pistol once and come off best. What a fool he had been, though, to let Carlsen regain his automatic! Now he was anxious for the landfall, keen for the show-down.

Far on the horizon, northward, he sighted glimmering flashes of milky whiteness that came and went to the swing of the schooner. This could not be land, he decided, or they would have announced it. It was ice, pack-ice, or floes. He tried to recollect all that he had heard or read of Arctic voyages, and succeeded only in comprehending his own ignorance. Of the rapidly changing conditions the commonest sailor aboard knew more than he. Blind Lund, sniffing to windward, smelled and heard far more than he could rightfully imagine.

Tamada appeared and announced breakfast.

"You'll be coming later, Rainey?" asked Carlsen. "You and Lund?"

He started for the companionway and the girl followed. As she passed the wheel Rainey spoke to her:

"I am sorry your father is worse, Miss Simms," he said.

She looked at him with eyes that were filled with sadness, that seemed liquid with tears bravely held back.

"I am afraid he is dying," she answered in a low voice. "Thank you, for you sympathy. I — "

She stopped at some slight sound that Rainey did not catch. But he saw the face of Carlsen framed in the shadow of the companion, his mouth open in the wolf grin, and the man's eyes were gleaming crimson. He held up a hand for the girl. She passed down without taking it.

Lund came over to Rainey.

"Clear weather, they tell me?" he said. "That's unusual. Fog off the Aleutians three hundred an' fifty days of the year, as a rule. Soon as we sight land, which'll be Unalaska or thereabouts, he'll have the course changed. There's a considerable fleet of United States revenue cutters at Unalaska, an' Carlsen won't pull ennything until we're well west of there. He's pretty cocky this mornin'. Wal, we'll see."

There had always been a certain rollicking good-humor about Lund. This morning he was grim, his face, with its beak of a nose and aggressive chin beneath the flaming whiskers, and his whole magnificent body gave the impression of resolve and repressed action. Rainey fancied whimsically that he could hear a dynamo purring inside of the giant's massiveness. He had seen him in open rage when he had first denounced Honest Simms, but the serious mood was far more impressive.

The big man stepped like a great cat, his head was thrust slightly forward, his great hands were half open. One forgot his blindness. Despite the unsightly black lenses, Lund appeared so absolutely prepared and, in a different way, fully as confident as Carlsen. A certain audacious assurance seemed to ooze out of him, to permeate his neighborhood, and a measure of it extended to Rainey.

"We'll sight Makushin first," muttered Lund, as if to himself.

"Makushin?"

"Volcano, fifty-seven hundred feet high. Much ice in sight?"

Rainey described the horizon.

"All fresh-water ice," said Lund. "An' melting."

"Melting? It must be way below freezing," said Rainey. Lund chuckled.

"This ain't cold, matey. Wait till we git *north*. Never saw it lower than five above in Unalaska in my life. It's the rainiest spot in the U. S. A. Rains two days out of three, reg'lar. This ice is comin' out of the strait. Sure sign it's breakin' up. The winter freeze ain't due for six weeks yet."

Carlsen, before he went below, had sent a man into the fore-spreaders, and now he shouted, cupping his hands and sounding his news as if it had been a call to arms.

"*Land-ho!*"

"What is it?" called Rainey back.

"High peak, sir. Dead ahead! Clouds on it, or smoke."

He came sliding down the halyards to the deck as Lund said: "That'll be Makushin. Now the fun'll commence."

From below the sailors off watch came up on deck, and the hunters, the latter wiping their mouths, fresh from their interrupted breakfast, all crowding forward to get a glimpse of the land. Rainey kept on the course, heading for the far-off volcano. Minutes passed before Carlsen came on deck. He had not hurried his meal.

"I'll take her over, Rainey," he said briefly.

Rainey and Lund were barely seated before the heeling of the schooner and the scuffle of feet told of Lund's prophesied change of course. Rainey looked at the telltale compass above his head.

"Heading due west," he told Lund.

"West it is," said the giant. "More coffee, Tamada. Fill your belly, Rainey. Get a good meal while the eatin' is good."

Although it was Hansen's watch below, Rainey found him at the wheel instead of the seaman he had left there. Carlsen came up to him smiling.

"Better let Hansen have the deck, Mr. Rainey," he said. "We're going to have a conference in the cabin at four bells, and I'd like you to be present."

"All right, sir," Rainey answered, getting a thrill at this first actual intimation of the meeting. Hansen, it seemed, was not to be one of the representatives of the seamen. And Carlsen had been smart enough to forestall Lund's demand for Rainey by taking some of the wind out of the giant's sails and doing the unexpected. Unless the hunters had suggested that Rainey be present. But that was hardly likely, considering that he was to be left out of the deal.

"In just what capacity are you callin' this conference?" Lund asked, when Carlsen notified him in turn. "The skipper ain't dead is he?"

"I represent the captain, Lund," replied the doctor. "He entirely approves of what I am about to suggest to you and the men. In fact I have his signature to a document that I hope you will sign also. It will be greatly to your interest to do so. I am in present charge of the *Karluk*."

"You ain't a reg'lar member of this expedition," objected Lund stolidly. "Neither am I a member of the crew, just now. But the skipper's my partner in this deal, signed, sealed and recorded. Afore I go to enny meetin' I'd like to have a talk with him personally. Thet's fair enough, ain't it?"

Several of the hunters had gathered about, and Lund's question seemed a general appeal. Carlsen shrugged his shoulders.

"If you had your eyesight," he said almost brutally, "you could soon see that the skipper was in no condition to discuss matters, much less be present."

"Here's my eyesight," countered Lund. "Mr. Rainey here. Let him see the skipper and ask him a question or two."

"What kind of question? I'm asking as his doctor, Lund."

"For one thing if he's read the paper you say he signed. I want to be sure of that. An' I don't make it enny of yore bizness, Carlsen, what I want to say to my partner, by proxy or otherwise. Second thing, I'd like to be sure he's still alive. As for yore standin' as his doctor, all I've got to say is that yo're a damned pore doctor, so fur as the skipper's concerned, ennyway."

The two men stood facing each other, Carlsen looking evilly at the giant, whose black glasses warded off his glance. It was wasting looks to glare at a blind man. Equally to sneer. But the bout between the two was timed now, and both were casting aside any veneer of diplomacy, their enmity manifesting itself in the raw. The issue was growing tense.

Rainey fancied that Carlsen was not entirely sure of his following, and relied upon Lund's indignant refusal of terms to back up his plans of getting rid of him decisively.

CHAPTER X
THE SHOW-DOWN

"Rainey can see the skipper," said Carlsen carelessly.

"All right," said Lund. "Will you do that, Rainey? Now?" And Rainey had a fleeting fancy that the giant winked one of his blind eyes at him, though the black lenses were deceiving.

He went below immediately and rapped on the door, a little surprised to see the girl appear in the opening. He had expected to find the skipper alone, and he was pretty sure that Carlsen had also expected this. The drawn expression of her face, the strained faint smile with which she greeted him, the hopeless look in her eyes, startled him.

"I wanted to see your father," he said in a low voice.

She told him to enter.

Captain Simms was lying in his bunk, apparently fully dressed, with the exception of his shoes. His cheeks had sunken, dark hollows showed under his closed eyes, the bones of his skull projected, and his flesh was the color of clay. Rainey believed that he was in the presence of death itself. He looked at the girl.

"He is in a stupor," she said. "He has been that way since last night, following a collapse. I can barely find his pulse, but his breath shows on this."

She produced a small mirror, little larger than a dollar, and held it before her father's lips. When she took it away Rainey saw a trace of moisture.

"Carlsen can not rouse him?" he asked.

"Can not — or will not," she answered in a voice that held a hard quality for all its despondency. Rainey glanced at the door. It was shut.

"What do you mean by that?" he asked, speaking low.

She looked at him as if measuring his dependency.

"I don't know," she answered dully. "I wish I did. Father's illness started with sciatica, through exposure to the cold and damp. It was better during the time the *Karluk* was in San Francisco though he had some severe attacks. He said that Doctor Carlsen gave him relief. I know that he did, for there were days at first when father had to stay in bed from the pain. It was in his left leg, and then it showed in frightful headaches, and he complained of pain about the heart. But he was bent on the voyage, and Doctor Carlsen guaranteed he could pull him through. But — lately — the doctor has seemed uncertain. He talks of perverted nerve functions, and he has obtained a tremendous influence over father.

"You heard what he said when — the night he tried to shoot you? You see, I am trusting you in all this, Mr. Rainey. I *must* trust some one. If I don't I can't stand it. I think I shall go mad sometimes. The doctor has changed. It is as if he was a dual personality — like Jekyll and Hyde — and now he is always Hyde. It is the gold that has turned his brain, his whole behavior from what he was in California before father returned and he learned of the island. He said last night that he could save father or — or — that he would let father die. I told him it was sheer murder! He laughed. He said he would save him — for a price."

She stopped, and Rainey supplied the gap, sure that he was right.

"If you would marry him?"

The girl nodded. "Father will do anything he tells him. I sometimes think he tortures father and only relieves him when father promises what he wants. Otherwise I could not understand. Last night father asked me to do this thing. Not because of any threat — he did not seem conscious of anything underhanded. He told me he looked upon the doctor as a son, that it would make him happy for me to marry him — now. That he would perform the ceremony. That he did not think he would live long and he wanted to see me with a protector.

"It was horrible. I dare not hint anything against the doctor. It brings on a nervous attack. Last night my refusal caused convulsions, and then — the collapse! What can I do? If I made the sacrifice how can I tell that Doctor Carlsen could — *would* save him? What shall I do?"

She was in an agony of self-questioning, of doubt.

"To see him lie there — like that. I can not bear it."

"Miss Simms," said Rainey, "your father is not in his right mind or he would see Carlsen as you do, as I do. Carlsen's brain is turned with the lure of the gold. If he marries you, I believe it is only for your share, for what you will get from your father. It can not be right to do a wrong thing. No good could come from it. But — something may happen this morning — I can not tell you what. I do not know, except that Lund is to face Carlsen. It may change matters."

"Lund," she said scornfully. "What can he do? And he accused my father of deserting him. I —"

A knock came at the door, and it started to open. Carlsen entered.

"Ah," he said. "I trust I have not disturbed you. I had no idea I should interrupt a tête-á-tête. Are you satisfied as to the captain's condition, Mr. Rainey?"

Rainey looked the scoffing devil full in his eyes, and hot scorn mounted to his own so swiftly that Carlsen's hand fell away from the door jamb toward his hip. Then he laughed softly.

"We may be able to bring him round, all right again, who knows?" he said.

Rainey went on deck, raging but impotent. He told Lund briefly of the talk between him and Peggy Simms, and described the general symptoms of the skipper's strange malady. It was nine o'clock, an hour to the meeting. He went down to his own room and sat on the bunk, smoking, trying to piece up the puzzle. If Carlsen was a potential murderer, if he intended to let Simms die, why should he want to marry the girl? He thought he solved that issue.

As his wife Carlsen would retain her share. If he gave her up, it would go into the common purse. But, if he expected to trick the men out of it all, that would be unnecessary. Did he really love the girl? Or was his lust for gold mingled with a passion for possession of her? He might know that the girl would kill herself before she would submit to dishonor. Perhaps he knew she had the means!

One thing became paramount. To save Peggy Simms. Lund might fight for the gold; Rainey would battle for the girl's sanctity. And, armed with that resolve, Rainey went out into the main cabin.

Carlsen took the head of the table. Lund faced him at the other end. All six of the hunters, as privileged characters, were present, but only three of the seamen, awkward and diffident at being aft. The nine, with Rainey, ranged themselves on either side of the table, five and five, with Rainey on Lund's right.

Tamada had brought liquor and glasses and cigars, and gone forward. The door between the main cabin and the corridor leading to the galley was locked after him by Deming. The girl was not present. Yet her share was an important factor.

Lund sat with folded arms, his great body relaxed. Now that the table was set, the cards all dealt, and the first play about to be made, the giant shed his tenseness. Even his grim face softened a trifle. He seemed to regard the affair with a certain amount of humor, coupled with the zest of a gambler who loves the game whether the stakes are for death or dollars.

Carlsen had a paper under his hand, but deferred its reading until he had addressed the meeting.

"A ship," he said, "is a little community, a world in itself. To its safety every member is a necessity, the lookout as much as the man at the wheel, the common seaman, the navigator. And, when a ship is engaged in a certain calling, those who are hired as experts in that line are equally essential with the rest."

"All the way from captain to — cook?" drawled Lund.

"Each depends upon his comrade's fulfilment of duty," went on Carlsen. "So an absolute equality is evolved. Each man's responsibility being equal, his reward should be also equal. It seems to me that this status of affairs is arrived at more naturally aboard the *Karluk* than it might be elsewhere. We are a small company, and not easily divided. The will of the majority may easily become that of all, may easily be applied.

"Payment for all services comes on this voyage from an uncertain amount of gold that Nature, Mother of us all, and therefore intending that all her children shall share her heritage, has washed up on a beach from some deep-sea vein and thus deposited upon an uncharted, unclaimed island. It is discovered by an Indian, the discovery is handed on to another."

"Meanin' me." Lund seemed to be enjoying himself. Despite the fact that Carlsen was presiding and most evidently assumed the attributes of leader, despite the fact that ten of the twelve at the table were arrayed against him, with the rest of the seamen behind them, Lund was decidedly enjoying himself.

To Rainey, the matter of the gold was but a mask for the license that would inevitably be manifested in such a crude democracy if it was established, a license that threatened the girl, now, he imagined, watching her father, the captain of the vessel, tottering on the verge of death. His pulses raced, he longed for the climax.

"This gold," went on Carlsen, "is not a commodity made in a factory, obtained through the toil of others, through the expenditure of capital. If it were, it would not alter the principle of the thing. It is of nature's own providing for those of her sons who shall find it and gather it. Sons that, as brothers, must willingly share and share alike."

Lund yawned, showing his strong teeth and the red cavern of his mouth. The hunters gazed at him curiously. The seamen, lacking initiative, lacking imagination, a crude collection of water-front drifters, more or less wrecked specimens of humanity who went to sea because they had no other capacity — were apathetic, listening to Carlsen with a sort of awe, a hypnosis before his argument that street rabble exhibit before the jargon of a soap-box orator.

Carlsen promised them something, therefore they followed him. But the hunters, more independent, more intelligent, seemed expecting an outburst from Lund and, because it was not forthcoming, they were a little uneasy.

"Share and share alike," said Lund. "I've got yore drift, Carlsen. Let's get down to brass tacks. The idea is to divvy the gold into equal parts, ain't it? How does she split? There's twenty-five souls aboard. Does that mean you split the heap into a hundred parts an' each one gits four?"

"No." It was Deming who answered. "It don't. The Jap don't come in, for one."

"A cook ain't a brother?"

"Not when he's got a yellow skin," answered Deming. "We'll take up a collection for Sandy. Rainey ain't in on the deal. We split it just twenty-two ways. What have you got to say about it?"

His tone was truculent, and Carlsen did not appear disposed to check him. He appeared not quite certain of the temper of the hunters. Deming, like Rainey, evidently chafed under the preliminaries.

"You figger we're all equal aboard," said Lund slowly, "leavin' out Mr. Rainey, Tamada an' Sandy. You an' me, an' Carlsen an' Harris there" — he nodded toward one of the seaman delegates who listened with his slack mouth agape, scratching himself under the armpit — "are all equal?"

Deming cast a glance at Harris and, for just a moment, hesitated.

Harris squirming under the look of Deming, which was aped by the sudden scrutiny of all the hunters, found speech: "How in hell did you know I was here?" he demanded of Lund. "I ain't opened my mouth yit!"

"That ain't the truth, Harris," replied Lund composedly. "It's allus open. But if you want to know, I smelled ye."

There was a guffaw at the sally. Carlsen's voice stopped it.

"I'll answer the question, Lund. Yes, we're all equal. The world is not a democracy. Harris, so far, hasn't had a chance to get the equal share that belongs to him by rights. That's what I meant by saying that the *Karluk* was a little world of its own. We're all equal on board."

"Except Rainey, Tamada an' Sandy. Seems to me yore argumint's got holes in it, Carlsen."

"We are waiting to know whether you agree with us?" replied Carlsen. His voice had altered quality. It held the direct challenge. Lund accepted it.

"I don't," he answered dryly. "There ain't enny one of you my equal, an' you've showed it. There ain't enny one of you, from Carlsen to Harris, who'd have the nerve to put it up to me alone. You had to band together in a pack, like a flock of sheep, with Carlsen for sheepherder.

I'm talking," he went on in a tone that suddenly leaped to thunder. "None of you have got the brains of Carlsen, becoz he had to put this scheme inter yore noddles. Deming, you think yo're a better man than Harris, you know damn' well you play better poker than the rest, an' you agreed to this becoz you figger you'll win most of the gold afore the v'yage is over. The rest of you suckers listened becoz some one tells you you are goin' to get more than what's rightly comin' to you.

"This gold is mine by right of discovery. I lose my ship through bad luck, an' I make a deal whereby the skipper gets the same as I do, an' the ship, which is the same as his daughter, gets almost as much. You men were offered a share on top of yore wages if you wanted to take the chance — two shares to the hunters. It was damned liberal, an' you grabbed at it. I got left on the ice, blind on a breakin' floe, an' you sailed off an' grabbed a handful or so of gold, enough to set you crazy.

"What in blazes would you know what to do with it, enny of you? Spill it all along the Barb'ry Coast, or gamble it off to Deming. Is there one of you 'ud have got off thet floe an', blind as I was, turned up ag'in? Not one of ye. An' when I *did* show you got sore becoz you'd figgered there 'ud be more with me away.

"A fine lot of skunks. You can take yore damned bit of paper an' light yore pipes with it, for all of me. To hell with it!

"*Shut up!*" His voice topped the murmurs at the table. Rainey saw Carlsen sitting back with his tongue-tip showing in a grin, tapping the table with the folded paper in one hand, the other in his lap, leaning back a little. He was like a man waiting for the last bet to be made before he exposed the winning hand.

"As for bein' equal, I've told you Carlsen's got the brains of you all. The skipper's dyin', Carlsen expects to marry his gal. An' he figgers thet way on pullin' down three shares to yore one. You say Rainey ain't in on the deal. He's as much so as Carlsen. Carlsen butts in as a doctor an' a fine job he's made of it. Skipper nigh dead. A hell of a doctor! Smoke up, all of you."

Carlsen sat quiet, sometimes licking his lips gently, listening to Lund as he might have listened to the rantings of a melodramatic actor. But Rainey sensed that he was making a mistake. He was letting Lund go too far. The men were listening to Lund, and he knew that the giant was talking for a specific purpose. Just to what end he could not guess. The big booming voice held them, while it lashed them.

"Equal to me? Bah! I'm a *man*. Yo're a lot of fools. Talk about me bein' blind. It was ice-blink got me. Then ophthalmy matterin' up my eyes. It's gold-blink's got you. Yo're cave-fish, a lot of blind suckers."

He leaned over the table pointing a massive square finger, thatched with red wool, direct at Carlsen, as if he had been leveling a weapon.

"Carlsen's a fake! He's got you hipped. He thinks he's boss, becoz he's the only navigator of yore crowd. I ain't overlooked that card, Carlsen. That ain't the only string he's got on ye. Nor the three shares he expects to pull down. He made you pore suckers fire off all your shells; he found out you ain't got a gun left among you that's enny more use than a club. He's got a gun an' he showed you how he could use it. He's sittin' back larfin' at the bunch of you!"

The men stirred. Rainey saw Carlsen's grin disappear. He dropped the paper. His face paled, the veins showed suddenly like purple veins in dirty marble.

"I've got that gun yet, Lund," he snarled.

Lund laughed, the ring of it so confident that the men glanced from him to Carlsen nervously.

"Yo're a fake, Carlsen," he said. "And I've got yore number! To hell with you an' yore popgun. You ain't even a doctor. I saw real doctors ashore about my eyes. Niphablepsia, they call snow-blindness. I'll bet you never heard of it. Yo're only a woman-conning dope-shooter! Else you'd have known that niphablepsia ain't *permanent*! I've bin' gettin' my sight back ever sence I left Seattle. An' now, damn you for a moldy hearted, slimy souled fakir, stand up an' say yo're my equal!"

He stood up himself, towering above the rest as they rose from their chairs, tearing the black glasses from his eyes and flinging them at Carlsen, who was forced to throw up a hand to ward them off. Rainey got one glimpse of the giant's eyes. They were gray-blue, the color of agate-ware, hard as steel, implacable.

Carlsen swept aside the spectacles and they shattered on the floor as he leaped up and the automatic shone in his hand. Lund had folded his arms above his great chest. He laughed again, and his arms opened.

In an instant Rainey caught the object of Lund's speech-making. He had done it to enrage Carlsen beyond endurance, to make him draw his gun. Giant as he was, he moved with the grace of a panther, with a swiftness too fast for the eye to register. Something flashed in his right hand, a gun, that he had drawn from a holster slung over his left breast.

The shots blended. Lund stood there erect, uninjured. A red blotch showed between Carlsen's eyes. He slumped down into his chair, his arms clubbing the table, his gun falling from his nerveless hand, his forehead striking the wood like the sound of an auctioneer's gavel. Lund had beaten him to the draw.

Lund, no longer a blind Samson, with contempt in his agate eyes, surveyed the scattering group of men who stared at the dead man dully, as if gripped by the exhibition of a miracle.

"It's all right, Miss Simms," he said. "Jest killed a skunk. Rainey, git that gun an' attend to the young lady, will you?"

The girl stood in the doorway of her father's cabin, her face frozen to horror, her eyes fixed on Lund with repulsion. As Rainey got the automatic, slipped it into his pocket, and went toward her, she shrank from him. But her voice was for Lund.

"You murderer!" she cried.

Lund grinned at her, but there was no laughter in his eyes.

"We'll thrash that out later, miss," he said. "Now, you men, jump for'ard, all of you. Deming, unlock that door. *Jump!* Equals, are you? I'll show you who's master on this ship. Wait!"

His voice snapped like the crack of a whip and they all halted, save Deming, who sullenly fitted the key to the lock of the corridor entrance.

"Take this with you," said Lund, pointing to Carlsen's sagging body. "When you git tired of his company, throw him overboard. Jump to it!"

The nearest men took up the body of the doctor and they all filed forward, silently obedient to the man who ordered them.

"They ain't all whipped yit," said Lund. "Not them hunters. They're still sufferin' from gold-blink, but I'll clean their eyesight for 'em. Look after the lady an' her father, Rainey."

Tamada entered as if nothing had happened. He carried a tray of dishes and cutlery that he laid down on the table.

"Never mind settin' a place for Carlsen, Tamada," said Lund. "He's lost his appetite — permanent." The Oriental's face did not change.

"Yes, sir," he answered.

The girl shuddered. Rainey saw that Lund was exhilarated by his victory, that the primitive fighting brute was prominent. Carlsen had tried to shoot first, goaded to it; his death was deserved; but it seemed to Rainey that Lund's exhibition of savagery was unnecessary. But he also saw that Lund would not heed any protest that he might make, he was still swept on by his course of action, not yet complete.

"I'll borrow Carlsen's sextant," said Lund. "Nigh noon, an' erbout time I got our reckonin'." He went into the doctor's cabin and came out with the instrument, tucking it under his arm as he went on deck.

Tamada went stolidly on with his preparations. He paused at the little puddle of blood where Carlsen's head had struck the table, turned, and disappeared toward his galley, promptly emerging with a wet cloth.

The girl put her hands over her eyes as Tamada methodically mopped up the telltale stains.

"The brute!" she said. Then took away her hands and extended them toward Rainey.

"What will he do with my father?" she said. "He thinks that dad deserted him. And the doctor, who might have saved him, is dead. My God, what shall I do? What shall I do?"

Rainey found himself murmuring some attempts at consolation, a defense of Lund.

"You too?" she said with a contempt that, unmerited as it was, stung Rainey to the quick. "You are on his side. Oh!"

She wheeled into her father's room and shut the door. Rainey heard the click of the bolt on the other side. Tamada was going on with his table-laying. Rainey saw that he had left Carlsen's place vacant. He listened for a moment, but heard nothing within the skipper's cabin. The swift rush of events was still a jumble. Slowly he went up the companionway to the deck.

CHAPTER XI
HONEST SIMMS

Lund greeted Rainey with a curt nod. Hansen was still at the helm. The crew on duty were standing about alert, their eyes on Lund. They had found a new master, and they were cowed, eager to do their best.

"It ain't noon yet," said Lund. "I hardly need to shoot the sun with the land that close."

Rainey looked over the starboard bow to where a series of peaks and lower humps of dark blue proclaimed the Aleutian island bridge stretching far to the west.

"I'll show this crew they've got a skipper aboard," said Lund. "How's the cap'en?"

Rainey told him.

"We'll see what we can do for him," said Lund. "He's better off without that fakir, that's a cinch. Called me a murderer," he went on with a good-humored laugh. "Got spunk, she has. And she's a trim bit. A slip of a gal, but she's game. An' good-lookin' eh, Rainey?"

He shot a keen glance at the newspaperman.

"You're in her bad hooks, too, ain't ye? We'll fix that after a bit. She don't know when she's well off. Most wimmin don't. An' she's the sort that needs handlin' right. She's upset now, natural, an' she hates me."

He smiled as if the prospect suited him. A suspicion leaped into Rainey's brain. Lund had said he would not see a decent girl harmed. But the man was changed. He had fought and won, and victory shone in his eyes with a glitter that was immune from sympathy, for all his air of good-nature.

He had said that a man under his skin was just an animal. His appraisal of the girl struck Rainey with apprehension. "To the victor belong the spoils." Somehow the quotation persisted. What if Lund regarded the girl as legitimate loot? He might have talked differently beforehand, to assure himself of Rainey's support.

And Rainey suddenly felt as if his support had been uncalled upon, a frail reed at best. Lund had not needed him, would he need him, save as an aid, not altogether necessary, with Hansen aboard, to run the ship?

He said nothing, but thrust both hands into the side pockets of the pilot coat he had acquired from the ship's stores. The sudden touch of cold steel gave him new courage. He had sworn to protect the girl. If Lund, seeming more like a pirate than ever, with his cold eyes sweeping the horizon, his bulk casting Rainey's into a dwarf's by comparison, attempted to harm Peggy Simms, Rainey resolved to play the part of champion.

He could not shoot like Lund, but he was armed. There were undoubtedly more cartridges in the clip. And he must secure the rest from Carlsen's cabin immediately.

The sun reached its height, and Lund busied himself with his sextant. Rainey determined to ask him to teach him the use of it. His consent or refusal would tell him where he stood with Lund.

He felt the mastery of the man. And he felt incompetent beside him. Carlsen had been right. A ship at sea was a little world of its own, and Lund was now lord of it. A lord who would demand allegiance and enforce it. He held the power of life and death, not by brute force alone. He was the only navigator aboard, with the skipper seriously ill. As such alone he held them in his hand, once they were out of sight of land.

"Hansen," said Lund, "Mr. Rainey'll relieve you after we've eaten. Come on, Rainey. You ain't lost yore appetite, I hope. Watch me discard that spoon for a knife an' fork. I don't have to play blind man enny longer."

Food did not appeal to Rainey. He could not help thinking of the spot under the cloth where Tamada had wiped up the blood of the man just killed by Lund, sitting opposite him, making play for a double helping of victuals.

It was Lund's apparent callousness that affected him more than his own squeamishness. He could not regret Carlsen's death. With the doctor alive, his own existence would have been a constant menace. But he was not used to seeing a killing, though, in his water-front detail, he had not been unacquainted with grim tragedies of the sea.

It was Lund's demeanor that gripped him. The giant had dismissed Carlsen as unceremoniously as he might have flipped the ash from a cigar, or tossed the stub overside.

"I've got to tackle those hunters," Lund said. "I expect trouble there, sooner or later. But I'm goin' to lay down the law to 'em. If they come clean, well an' good, they git their original two shares. If not, they don't get a plugged nickel. An' Deming's the one who'll stir up the trouble, take it from me. Tell Hansen to turn in his watch-off, I shan't take a deck for a day or two, you'll have to go on handlin' it between you. I've got to make my peace with the gal, an' do what I can with the skipper."

"She'll not make peace easily. But the skipper's in a bad way."

Lund lit his pipe.

"I'd jest as soon it was war. I don't see as we can help the skipper much 'less we try reverse treatment of what Carlsen did. If we knew what that was? If he gits worse she'll let us know, I reckon. Mebbe you can suggest somethin'?"

Rainey shook his head.

"I suppose she can do more than any of us," he said.

Lund nodded, then whistled to Tamada, leaving the cabin.

"Take a bottle of whisky to the hunters' mess, with my compliments. That'll give 'em about three jolts apiece," he said to Rainey. "Long as we've won out we may as well let 'em down easy. But they'll work for their shares, jest the same. A drink or two may help 'em swaller what I'm goin' to give 'em by way of dessert in the talkin' line. See you later."

Rainey took the dismissal and went up to the relief of Hansen. He did not mention what had happened until the Scandinavian referred to it indirectly.

"They put the doc overboard, sir, soon's Mr. Lund an' you bane go below."

It seemed a summary dismissal of the dead, without ceremony. Yet, for the rite to be authentic, Lund must have presided, and the sea-burial service would have been a mockery under the circumstances. It was the best thing to have done, Rainey felt, but he could not avoid a mental shiver at the thought of the man, so lately vital, his brain alive with energy, sliding through the cold water to the ooze to lie there, sodden, swinging with the sub-sea currents until the ocean scavengers claimed him.

"All right, Hansen," he said in answer, and the man hurried off after his extra detail.

Lund came up after a while, and Rainey told him of the fate of Carlsen's body.

"I figgered they'd do about that," commented Lund. "They savvied he'd aimed to make suckers out of 'em, an' they dumped him. But they ain't on our side, by a long sight. Not that I give a damn. If they want to sulk, let 'em sulk. But they'll stand their watches, an', when we git to the beach, they'll do their share of diggin'. If they need drivin', I'll drive 'em.

"That Deming is a better man than I thought. He's the main grouch among 'em. Said if I hadn't had a gun he'd have tackled me in the cabin. Meant it, too, though I'd have smashed him. He's sore becoz I said he warn't my equal. I told him, enny time he wanted to try it out, I'd accommodate him. He didn't take it up, an' they'll kid him about it. He'll pack a grudge. I ain't afraid of their knifin' me, not while the skipper's sick. They need me to navigate."

"This might be a good chance for me to handle a sextant," suggested Rainey casually.

Lund shook his head, smiling, but his eyes hard.

"Not yet, matey," he said. "Not that I don't trust you, but for me to be the only one, jest now, is a sort of life insurance that suits me to carry. They might figger, if you was able to navigate, that they c'ud put the screws on you to carry 'em through, with me out of the way. I don't say they could, but they might make it hard for you, an' you ain't got quite the same stake in this I have."

Here was cold logic, but Rainey saw the force of it. Hansen came up early to split the watch and put their schedule right again, and Lund went below with Rainey. Lund ordered Tamada to bring a bottle and glasses, and they sat down at the table. Rainey needed the kick of a drink, and took one.

As Lund was raising his glass with a toast of "Here's to luck," the skipper's door opened and the girl appeared. She looked like a ghost. Her hair was disheveled and her eyes stared at them without seeming recognition. But she spoke, in a flat toneless voice.

"My father is dead! I — " she faltered, swayed, and seemed to swoon as she sank toward the floor. Rainey darted forward, but Lund was quicker and swooped her up in his arms as if she had been a feather, took her to the table, set her in a chair, dabbled a napkin in some water and applied it to her brows.

"Chafe her wrists," he ordered Rainey. "Undo that top button of her blouse. That's enough; she ain't got on corsets. She'll come through. Plumb worn out. That's all."

He handled her, deftly, as a nurse would a child. Rainey chafed the slender wrists and beat her palms, and soon she opened her eyes and sighed. Then she pulled away from Lund, bending over her, and got to her feet.

"I must go to my father," she said. "He is dead."

They followed her into the cabin, and Lund bent over the bunk.

"Looks like it," he whispered to Rainey. Then he tore open the skipper's vest and shirt and laid his head on his chest. The girl made a faint motion as if to stop him, but did not hinder him. She was at the end of her own strength from weariness and worry. Lund suddenly raised his head.

"There's a flutter," he announced. "He ain't gone yit. Get Tamada an' some brandy."

The Japanese, by some intuition, was already on hand, and produced the brandy. Rainey poured out a measure. The captain's teeth were tightly clenched. Lund spraddled one great hand across his jaws, pressing at their junction, forcing them apart, firmly, but gently enough, while Rainey squeezed in a few drops of brandy from the corner of his soaked handkerchief. Lund stroked the sick man's throat, and he swallowed automatically.

"More brandy," ordered Lund.

With the next dose there came signs of revival, a low moan from the skipper. The girl flew to his side. Tamada, standing by with the bottle, stepped forward, handed the brandy to Rainey, and rolled up the lid of an eye, looking closely at the pupil.

"I study medicine at Tokio," he said.

"Why didn't ye say so before?" demanded Lund. It did not occur to any of them to doubt Tamada's word. There was an air of professional assurance and an efficiency about him that carried weight. "What can you do for him? There's a medicine chest in Carlsen's room."

"I was hired to cook," said Tamada quietly. "I should not have been permit to interfere. It is not my business if a white man makes a fool of himself. Now we want morphine and hypodermic syringe."

Tamada rolled up the captain's sleeve. The flesh, shrunken, pallid, was closely spotted with dot-like scars that showed livid, as if the captain had been suffering from some strange rash.

Lund whistled softly. Rainey, too, knew what it meant. The skipper had been a veritable slave to the drug. Carlsen had administered it, prescribed it, used it as a means to bring Simms under his subjection. The girl looked strangely at Tamada.

"Would he have taken that for sciatica?" she asked.

"I think, perhaps, yes. Injection over muscle gives relief. Sometimes makes cure. But Captain Simms take too much. Suppose this supply cut off very suddenly, then come too much chills, maybe collapse, maybe — " The girl clutched his arm.

"You meant more than you said. It might mean death?"

"I don't know," replied Tamada gravely. "Perhaps, if now we have morphine, presently we give him smaller dose every time, it will be all right." He lifted up the sick man's hand and examined the nails critically. They were broken, brittle.

Rainey had gone to Carlsen's room in search of the drug and the injecting needle.

"How much d'ye suppose he took at once?" Lund asked the Japanese in a low voice.

"Fifteen grains, I think. Maybe more. Too much! Always too much drug in his veins. Much worse than opium for man."

"Carlsen's work," growled Lund. "Increased the stuff on him till he couldn't do without it. Made him a slave to dope an' Carlsen his boss. He deserved killin' jest for that, the skunk."

Rainey frantically searched through the medicine chest and, finding only five tablets marked *Morphine 1 gr.* in a bottle, sought elsewhere in vain. And he could find no needle. But he ran across some automatic cartridges and put them in his pockets before he hurried back.

"This is not enough," said Tamada. "And we should have needle. But I dissolve these in galley." And he hurried out. The girl had slipped down on her knees beside the bed, holding her father's hand against her lips, her eyes closed. She seemed to be praying.

Rainey and Lund looked at each other. Rainey was trying to recall something. It came at last, the memory of Carlsen slipping something in his pocket as he had come out of the captain's room. That had been the hypodermic case! As the thought lit up' his eyes he saw a flash in Lund's.

"Carlsen had the morphine on him," said Lund in a whisper, not to disturb the girl.

"And the needle!" said Rainey. "What if?" He raced out of the cabin forward, passing Tamada, coming out of the galley with the dissolved tablets in a glass that steamed with hot water. Swiftly he told his suspicions.

"They may have searched him first," he said, and went on to the hunters' cabin. They were seated about their table, talking. On seeing Rainey they stopped abruptly and viewed him suspiciously. Deming rose.

"What's the idea?" he asked and his tone was not friendly.

Rainey hurriedly explained. Deming shrugged his shoulders.

"They sewed him up in canvas in the fo'k'le," he said indifferently. "None of us went through him. I think they made the kid do the job."

Rainey found Sandy in his bunk, asleep, trying to get one of the catnaps by which he made up his lack of definitely assigned rest. The roustabout woke with a shudder, flinching under Rainey's hand.

"They made me do it," he said in answer. "None of 'em 'ud touch it till I had it sewed in an old staysail, an' a boatkedge tied on for weight. I didn't go inter his pockets. I was scared to touch it more'n I had to."

"Is that the truth, Sandy? I don't care what you took besides this little case and a bottle of tablets. You can keep the rest."

"It's the bloody truth, Mister Rainey, s'elp me," whined Sandy. And the truth was in his shifty eyes.

Rainey went back with his news. He imagined that the five grains would prove temporarily sufficient. And they could put in for Unalaska. There were surgeons there with the revenue fleet. He thought there was probably a hospital.

They would have to explain Carlsen's death. They would be asked about the purpose of the voyage, the crew examined. It might mean detention, the defeat of the expedition, the very thing that Lund had feared, the following of them to the island. He wondered how Lund would take to the plan.

He found that Tamada had administered the morphine. Already the beneficial results were apparent. The dry, frightfully sallow skin had changed and Simms was breathing freely while Tamada, feeling his pulse, nodded affirmatively to the girl's questioning glance.

"Got it?" asked Lund.

Rainey gave the result of his search.

"We'll have to put in to Unalaska," he said. "There are doctors there." The girl turned toward Lund. He smiled at the intensity of her gaze and pose.

"I play fair, Miss Peggy," he said. "Rainey, change the course."

Peggy Simms seized Lund's great paw in both her hands, and, for the first time, the tears overflowed her eyes. The *Karluk* came about as Rainey reached the deck and gave his orders. Then he returned to the cabin. The captain had opened his eyes.

"Peggy!" he murmured. "Carlsen, where is he? Lund! Good God, Lund, you can see?"

"Keep quiet as you can," said Tamada. Something in his voice made the skipper shift his look to the Japanese.

"Where's Carlsen?" he asked again.

"He can't come now," said Tamada.

Under the urge of the drug the skipper's brain seemed abnormally clear, his intuition heightened.

"Carlsen's dead?" he asked. Then, shifting to Lund. "You killed him, Jim?"

Lund nodded.

"How much morphine did you give me?"

"Five grains."

"It's not enough. It won't last. *There isn't any more?*" he flashed out, with sudden energy, trying to raise himself.

"We're puttin' in for Unalaska, Simms," said Lund.

"How far?"

"'Bout seventy miles."

"Then it's too late. Too late. The pain's shifted of late — to my heart. It'll get me presently."

The girl darted a look of hate at Lund, an accusation that he met composedly, swift as the change had come from the almost reverence with which she had clasped his hand.

"I'll be gone in an hour or two," said the skipper. "Got to talk while this lasts. Jim — about leavin' you that time. I could have come back. I had words about it — with Hansen. He knows. But the gale was bad, an' the ice. It wasn't the gold, Jim. I swear it. I had the ship an' crew to look out for. An' Peggy, at home.

"I might have gone back sooner, Jim, I'll own up to that. But it wasn't the gold that did it. An' — I didn't hear what you shouted, Jim. The storm came up. We were frozen by the time we found the ship. Numb.

"Then, then; oh, God, my heart!" He sat upright, clutching at his chest, his face convulsed with spasms of pain. Tamada got some brandy between the chattering teeth. Sweat poured out on the skipper's forehead, and he sank back, exhausted but temporarily relieved. The girl wiped his brows.

"It'll get me next attack," he said presently in a weak voice. "Jim, this trouble hit me the day after we left the floe. Not sciatica, at first, but in the head. I couldn't think right. I was just numb in the brain. An' when it cleared off, it was too late. The ice had closed. We couldn't go back. I read up in my medical book, Jim, later, when the sciatica took me.

"Had to take to my bunk. Couldn't stand. I had morphine, an' it relieved me. Took too much after a while. Had to have it. Got better in San Francisco for a bit. Then Carlsen prescribed it. Morphine was my boss, an' then Carlsen, he was boss of the morphine. Seemed like — seemed like — *More brandy, Tamada.*"

His voice was weaker when he spoke again. They came closer to catch his whispers.

"Carlsen — mind wasn't my own. Peggy — I wasn't in my right mind, honey. Not when — Carlsen — he was angel when he gave me what I wanted — devil — when he wouldn't. Made me — do things. But he's dead. And I'm going. Never reach Unalaska. Peggy — forgive. Meant for best — but — not in right mind. Jim — it wasn't the gold. Not Peggy's fault — anyway."

"She'll get hers, Simms," said Lund. "Yours too."

The skipper's eyes closed and his frame settled under the clothes. The girl flung herself on the bed in uncontrollable weeping. Lund raised his eyebrows at Tamada, who shrugged his shoulders.

"Better get out o' here," whispered Lund. He and Rainey went out together. In a few minutes Tamada joined them, his face sphinxlike as ever.

"He is dead," he said.

Rainey and Lund went on deck. The schooner thrashed toward the volcano, the bearing-mark for Unalaska, hidden behind it. They paced up and down in silence.

"I guess he was 'Honest Simms,' after all," said Lund at last. "The gal blames me for the morphine, but Carlsen never meant him to live. She'll see that after a bit, mebbe."

Rainey glanced at him curiously. He was getting fresh lights on Lund.

Then the girl appeared, pale, composed, coming straight up to Lund, who halted his stride at sight of her.

"Will you change the course, Mr. Lund?" she said.

He looked at her in surprise.

"Father spoke once more. After you left. He does not want you to go on to Unalaska. He said it would mean a rush for the gold; perhaps you would have to stay there. He does not want you to lose the gold. He wants me to have my share. He made me promise. And he wants — he wants" — she bit her lip fiercely in repression of her feelings — "to be buried at sea. That was his last request."

She turned and looked over the rail, struggling to wink back her tears. Rainey saw the giant's glance sweep over her, full of admiration.

"As you wish, Miss Peggy," he said. "Hansen, 'bout ship. Hold on a minnit. How about you, Miss Peggy? If you want to go home, we can find ways at Unalaska. I play fair. I'll bring back yore share — in full."

"I am not thinking about the gold," the girl said scornfully. "But I want to carry out my father's last wishes, if you will permit me. I shall stay with the ship. Now I am going back to him. You — you" — she quelled the tremble of her mouth, and her chin showed firm and determined — "you can arrange for the funeral to-morrow at dawn, if you will. I want him to-night."

Her face quivered piteously, but she conquered even that and walked to the companionway.

"Game, by God, game as they make 'em!" said Lund.

CHAPTER XII
DEMING BREAKS AN ARM

Rainey, dozing in his bunk, going over the sudden happenings of the day, had placed Carlsen's automatic under his pillow after loading it. He found that it lacked four shells of full capacity, the two that Lund had fired at his bottle target, the one fired by Carlsen at Rainey, and the last ineffective shot at Lund, a shot that went astray, Rainey decided, largely through Lund's *coup-de-theatre* of tearing off his glasses and flinging them at the doctor.

The dynamo that he had idly fancied he could hear purring away inside of Lund was apparent with vengeance now, driving with full force. That was what Lund would be from now on, a driver, imperative, relentless, overcoming all obstacles; as he had himself said, selfish at heart, keen for his own ends.

Rainey was neither a weakling nor a coward, but he shrank from open encounter with Lund, and knew himself, without fear, the weaker man. The challenge of Lund, splendidly daring any one of them to come out against him alone, and challenging them *en masse*, had found in Rainey an acknowledgment of inferiority that was not merely physical.

Lund knew far more than he did about the class of men that made up the inhabitants of the *Karluk*. Rainey had once fondly hugged the delusion that he knew something of the nature of those who "went down to the sea in ships."

Now he knew that his ignorance was colossal. Such men were not complex, they moved by instinct rather than reason, they were not guided by conscience, the values of right and wrong were not intuitive with them, muscle rather than mind ruled their universe.

Yet Rainey could not solve them, and Lund knew them as one may know a favorite book.

Lund had brains, cunning, brute force that commanded a respect not all bred of being weaker. In a way he was magnificent. And Rainey vaguely heralded trouble when Captain Simms was at last given to the deep. He felt certain that the hunters under Deming were hatching something but, in the main, his mental prophecy of trouble coming was connected with the girl.

Lund had shown no disrespect to her, rather the opposite. But the girl showed hatred of Lund and, in minor measure, of Rainey. Some of this would die out, naturally. Rainey intended to attempt an adjustment in his own behalf. But he held the feeling that Lund would not tolerate this hatred against him on the part of the girl. Such scorn would arouse something in the giant's nature, something that would either strike under the lash, or laugh at it.

Dimly, Rainey saw these things as the giant gropings of sex, not as he had known it, surrounded by conventionalities, by courtesies of twentieth-century veneering, but a law, primitive, irresistible, sweeping away barriers and opposition, a thing bigger even than the lust of gold; the lure of woman for man, and man for woman.

Both Lund and the girl, he felt, would have this thing in greater measure than he would. He shared his life with too many things, with books, with amusements, with the social ping-pong of the level in which he ordinarily moved.

There had been once a girl, perhaps there still was a girl, whom Rainey had known on a visit to the camp-palace of a lumber king, high in the Sierras, a girl who rode and hunted and lived out-of-doors, and yet danced gloriously, sang, sewed and was both feminine and masculine, a maddening latter-day Diana, who had swept Rainey off his feet for the time.

But he had known that he was not up to her standards, that he was but a paper-worm, aside from his lack of means. That latter detail would, he knew, have bothered him far more than her. But she announced openly that she would only mate with a man who had lived. He rather fancied that it had been a challenge — one he had not taken up. The matrix of his own life just then was too snug a bed. Well, he was living now, he told himself.

On the border of dreams he was brought back by a strange noise on deck, a rush of feet, many voices, and topping them all, the bellow of Lund, roaring, not for help, but in challenge.

Rainey, half asleep, jumped from his bunk and rushed out of the room. He had no doubt as to what had happened; the hunters had attacked Lund! And, unused to the possession of firearms, still drowsy, he forgot the automatic, intent upon rallying to the cry of the giant. As he made for the companionway, the girl came out of her father's room.

"What is it?" she cried.

"Lund — hunters!" Rainey called back as he sped up the stairs. He thought he heard a "wait" from her, but the stamping and yelling were loud in his ears, and he plunged out on deck. As he emerged he saw the stolid face of Hansen at the wheel, his pale blue eyes glancing at the set of his canvas and then taking on a glint as they turned amidships.

Lund looked like a bear surrounded by the dog-pack. He stood upright while the six hunters tore and smashed at him. Two had caught him by the middle, one from the front and one from the rear, and, as the fight raged back and forth, they were swung off their feet, bludgeoned and kicked by Lund to stop them getting at the gun in its holster slung under his coat close to his armpit.

Lund's arms swung like clubs, his great hands plucked at their holds, while he roared volleys of deep-sea, defiant oaths, shaking or striking off a man now and then, who charged back snarlingly to the attack.

Brief though the fight had been when Rainey arrived, there was ample evidence of it. Clothes were torn and faces bloody, and already the men were panting as Lund dragged them here and there, flailing, striking, half-smothered, but always coming up from under, like a rock that emerges from the bursting of a heavy wave.

And the voice of the combat, grunts and snarls, gasping shouts and broken curses, was the sound of ravening beasts. So far as Rainey could vision in one swift moment before he ran forward, no knives were being used.

A hunter lunged out heavily and confidently to meet him as the others got Lund to his knees for a fateful moment, piling on top of him, bludgeoning blows with guttural cries of fancied victory.

Rainey's man struck, and the strength of his arm, backed by his hurling weight, broke down Rainey's guard and left the arm numb. The next instant they were at close quarters, swinging madly, rife with the one desire to down the other, to maim, to kill. A blow crashed home on Rainey's cheek, sending him back dazed, striking madly, clinching to stop the piston-like smashes of the hunter clutching him, trying to trip him, hammering at the fierce face above him as they both went down and rolled into the scuppers, tearing at each other.

He felt the man's hands at his throat, gradually squeezing out sense and breath and strength, and threw up his knee with all his force. It struck the hunter fairly in the groin, and he heard the man groan with the sudden agony. But he himself was nearly out. The man seemed to fade away for the second, the choking fingers relaxed, and Rainey gulped for air. His eyes seemed strained from bulging from their sockets in that fierce grip, and there was a fog before them through which he could hear the roar of Lund, sounding like a siren blast that told he was still fighting, still confident.

Then he saw the hunter's face close to his again, felt the whole weight of the man crushing him, felt the bite of teeth through cloth and flesh, nipping down on his shoulder as the man lay on him, striving to hold him down until he regained the strength that the blow in the groin had temporarily broken down.

For just a moment Rainey's spirit sagged, his own strength was spent, his will sapped, his lungs flattened. For a moment he wanted to lie there — to quit.

Then the hunter's body tautened for action, and, at the feel, Rainey's ebbing pride came surging back, and he heaved and twisted, clubbing the other over his kidneys until the roll of the schooner sent them twisting, tumbling over to the lee once more.

He felt as if he had been fighting for an hour, yet it had all taken place during the leap of the *Karluk* between two long swells that she had negotiated with a sidelong lurch to the cross seas and wind.

Rainey came up uppermost. The hunter's head struck the rail heavily. His shoulder was free, but he could see ravelings of his coat in the other's teeth. The pain in his shoulder was evident enough, and the sight of the woolly fragments maddened him. The tactics of boyish fights came back to him, and he broke loose from the arms that hugged him, hitched forward until he sat on the hunter's chest, set a knee on either bicep and battered at the other's face as it twisted from side to side helplessly, making a pulp of it, keen to efface all semblance of humanity, a brute like the rest of them, intent upon bruising, on blood-letting, on beating all resistance down to a quivering, spirit-broken mass.

The hunter lay still beneath him at last, his nerve centers shattered by some blow that had short-circuited them, and Rainey got wearily to his feet. The hunter's thumbs had pressed deep on each side of his neck, and his head felt like wood for heaviness, but shot with pain. The vigor was out of him. He knew he could not endure another hand-to-hand battle with one of the crowd still raging about Lund, who was on his feet again.

Rainey saw his face, one red mask of blood and hair, with his agate eyes flaring up with the glory of the fight. He roared no longer, saving his breath. Hands clutched for him and fists fell, a man was tugging at each knee of his legs, set far apart, sturdy as the masts themselves.

Lund's arm came up, lifting a hunter clean from the deck, shook him off somehow, and crashed down. One of the men tackling his legs dropped senseless from the buffet he got on the side of his skull, and Lund's kick sent him scudding across the deck, limp, out of the fight that could not last much longer.

All this came as Rainey, still dazed, helped himself by the skylight toward the companion, going as fast as he could to get his gun. If he did not hurry he was certain they would kill Lund. No man could withstand those odds much longer.

And, Lund killed, hell would break loose. It would be his turn next, and the girl would be left at their mercy. The thought spurred him, cleared his throbbing head, jarred by the smashes of his still senseless opponent who would be coming to before long.

Then he saw the girl, standing by the rail, not crouching, as he had somehow expected her to be, shutting out the sight of the fight with trembling hands, but with her face aglow, her eyes shining, watching, as a Roman maid might have watched a gladiatorial combat; thrilled with the spectacle, hands gripping the rail, leaning a little forward.

She did not notice Rainey as he crept by Hansen, still guiding the schooner, holding her to her course, imperturbable, apparently careless of the issue. As he staggered down the stairs the line of thought he had pursued in his bunk, broken by the noise of the fight and his participation, flashed up in his brain.

This was sex, primitive, predominant! The girl must sense what might happen to her if Lund went down. She had no eyes for Rainey, her soul was up in arms, backing Lund. The shine in her eyes was for the strength of his prime manhood, matched against the rest, not as a person, an individual, but as an embodiment of the conquering male.

He got the gun, and he snatched a drink of brandy that ran through his veins like quick fire, revivifying him so that he ran up the ladder and came on deck ready to take a decisive hand.

But he found it no easy matter to risk a shot in that swirling mass. They all seemed to be arm weary. Blows no longer rose and fell. Lund was slowly dragging the dead weight of them all toward the mast. The two men on the deck still lay there. Rainey's opponent was trying to get up, wiping clumsily at the blood on his face, blinded.

The girl still stood by the rail. Back of the wrestling mass stood the seamen, offering to take no part, their arms aswing like apes, their dull faces working. Tamada stood by the forward companion, his arms folded, indifferent, neutral.

All this Rainey saw as he circled, while the mass whirled like a teetotum. The action raced like an overtimed kinetoscopic film. A man broke loose from the scrimmage, on the opposite side from Rainey, who barely recognized the disheveled figure with the bloody, battered face as Deming. The hunter had managed to get hold of Lund's gun. Rainey's aim was screened by a sudden lunge of the huddle of men. He saw Lund heave, saw his red face bob up, mouth open, roaring once more, saw his leg come up in a tremendous kick that caught Deming's outleveling arm close to the elbow, saw the gleam of the gun as it streaked up and overboard, and Deming staggering back, clutching at his broken limb, cursing with the pain, to bring up against the rail and shout to the seamen:

"Get into it, you damned cowards! Get into it, and settle him!"

Even in that instant the sarcasm of the cry of "cowards" struck home to Rainey. The next second the girl had jumped by him, a glint of metal in her hand as she brought it out of her blouse. This time she saw him. "Come on!" she cried. And darted between the fighters and the storming figure of Deming, who tried to grasp her with his one good arm, but failed.

Rainey sped after her just as Lund reached the mast. The girl had a nickeled pistol in her hand and was threatening the sullen line of irresolute seamen. Rainey with his gun was not needed. He heard Lund shout out in a triumphant cry and saw him battering at the heads of three who still clung to him.

All through the fight Lund had kept his head, struggling to the purpose he had finally achieved, to reach the mast-rack of belaying pins, seize one of the hardwood clubs and, with this weapon, beat his assailants to the deck.

He stood against the mast, his clothes almost stripped from him, the white of his flesh gleaming through the tatters, streaked with blood. Save for his eyes, his face was no longer human, only a mass of flayed flesh and clotted beard. But his eyes were alight with battle and then, as Rainey gazed, they changed. Something of surprise, then of delight, leaped into them, followed by a burning flare that was matched in those of the girl who, with Rainey herding back the seamen, had turned at Lund's yell of victory.

Lund took a lurching step forward over the prone bodies of the men on the deck, that was splotched with blood.

"By God!" he said slowly, his arms opening, his great fingers outspread, his gaze on the girl, "by God!"

The girl's face altered. Her eyes grew frightened, cold. The retreating blood left her cheeks pale, and she wheeled and fled, dodging behind Tamada, who gave way to let her pass, his ivory features showing no emotion, closing up the fore companionway as Peggy Simms dived below.

Lund did not follow her. Instead, he laughed shortly and appeared to see Rainey for the first time.

"Jumped me, the bunch of 'em!" he said, his chest heaving, his breath coming in spurts from his laboring lungs. "Couldn't use my gun. But I licked 'em. Damn 'em! *Equals?* Hell!"

He seemed to have a clear recollection of the fight. He smiled grimly at Deming, who glared at him, nursing his broken arm, then glanced at the man that Rainey had mastered.

"Did him up, eh? Good for you, matey! You didn't have to use your gun. Jest as well, you might have plugged me. An' the gal had one, after all."

He seemed to ruminate on this thought as if it gave him special cause for reflection.

"Game!" he said. "Game as they make 'em!"

He surveyed the rueful, groaning combatants with the smile of a conqueror, then turned to the seamen.

"Here, you!" he roared, and they jumped as if galvanized into life by the shout. "Chuck a bucket of water over 'em! Chuck water till they git below. Then clean the decks. Off-watch, you're out of this. Below with you, where you belong. Jump!"

"They all fought fair," he went on. "Not a knife out. Only Deming there, when he knew he was licked, tried to git my gun. Yo're yeller, Deming," he said, with contempt that was as if he had spat in the hunter's face. "I thought you were a better man than the rest. But you've got yores. Git down below an' we'll fix you up."

He strode over to Hansen, stolid at the wheel.

"Wal, you wooden-faced squarehead," he said, "which way did you think it was coming out? Damn me if you didn't play square, though! You kept her up. If you'd liked you could have chucked us all asprawl, an' that would have bin the end of it, with me down. You git a bottle of booze for that, Hansen, all for yore own Scandinavian belly. Come on, Rainey. Tamada, I want you."

While Tamada got splints and did what he could for the badly shattered arm, Lund taunted Deming until the hunter's face was seamed with useless ferocity, like a weasel's in a trap.

"I wonder you fix him at all, Tamada," he said. "He wanted to cut you out of yore share. Called you a yellow-skinned heathen, Tamada. What makes you gentle him that way? You've got him where you want him."

Tamada, binding up the splints professionally, looked at Deming with jetty eyes that revealed no emotion.

Lund passed his hand over his face.

"I'm some mess myself," he said, stretching his great arms. "Give me a five-finger drink, Rainey, afore I clean up. Some scrap. Hell popping on deck, and a dead man in the cabin! And the gal! Did you see the gal, Rainey?"

Out of the bloody mask of his face his agate eyes twinkled at Rainey with a sort of good-natured malice. Rainey did not answer as he poured the liquor.

"Make it four finger," exclaimed Lund. "Deming's goin' to faint. One for Doc Tamada."

The Japanese excused himself, helping Deming, worn out with pain and consumed by baffled hate, forward through the galley corridor. Then he came back with warm water in a basin — and towels.

"After this cheery little fracas," said Lund, mopping at his face, "we'll mebbe have a nice, quiet, genteel sort of ship. My gun went overboard, didn't it? Better let me have that one you've got, Rainey."

He stretched out his hand for it. Rainey delivered it, reluctantly. There was nothing else to do, but he felt more than ever that the *Karluk* was henceforth to be a one-man ship, run at the will of Lund.

But the girl, too, had a weapon. He hugged that thought. She carried it for her own protection, and she would not hesitate to use it. What a girl she was! What a woman rather! A woman who would *mate* — not marry for the quiet safety of a home. Rainey thought of her as one does of a pool that one plumbs with a stone, thinking to find it fairly shallow, only to discover it a gulf with unknown depth and currents, capable of smiling placidness or sudden storm.

CHAPTER XIII

THE RIFLE CARTRIDGES

The girl did not appear for the evening meal. She had refused Tamada's suggestions through the door. Lund drank heavily, but without any effect, save to sink him in comparative silence, as he and Rainey sat together, after the Japanese had cleared the table. In contrast to the excitement of the fight, their moods had changed, sobered by the thought of the girl sitting up with her dead in the captain's room.

Rainey was bruised and stiffened, and Lund moved with less of his usual ease. The flesh of his face had been so pounded that it was turning dull purple in great patches, giving him a diabolical appearance against his naming beard.

"We've got to git hold of those cartridges," he said, after a long-pause. "Carlsen had 'em planted somewhere, an' it's likely in his room. Best thing to do is to chuck 'em overboard. Cheaper to dump the cartridges an' shells than the rifles an' shotguns.

"You see," he went on, "Deming ain't quit. That's one thing with a man who's streaked with yeller, when he gits licked in the open an' knows he's licked proper, he tries to git even underhanded. He knows jest as well as I do that Carlsen was lyin' that time about there bein' no more shells. O' course the skipper may have stowed 'em away, but I doubt it. An' jest so long as he thinks there's a chance of gittin' at 'em, he'll figger on turning' the tables some day. An' he'll be workin' the rest of 'em up to the job."

"They can't do much without a navigator," suggested Rainey.

"Mebbe they figger a man'll do a lot o' things he don't want to with a rifle barrel stuck in his neck or the small of his back," said Lund grimly. "It's a good persuader. Might even have some influence on me. Then ag'in it might not."

"Where is the magazine?" asked Rainey.

"In the little room aft o' the galley. We'll look there first. Come on."

"How about keys? Carlsen's must have been in his pockets. I didn't see them when I was hunting the morphine. We can't go in there." Rainey made a motion toward the skipper's room. Lund chuckled.

"I had my keys to the safe an' the magazine when I was aboard last trip," he said. "They was with me when we went on the ice. An' I hung on to 'em. Allus thought I might have a chance to use 'em ag'in."

The strong room of the *Karluk* was a narrow compartment, heavily partitioned off from the galley and the corridor. There was a lamp there, and Rainey lit it while Lund closed the door behind them. The magazine was an iron chest fastened to the floor and the side of the vessel with two padlocks, opened by different keys. It was quite empty.

"Thorough man, Carlsen," said Lund. "Prepared for a show-down, if necessary. Might have put 'em in the safe. Wonder if he changed the combination? I bet Simms didn't, year in an' out."

He worked at the disk and grunted as the tumblers clicked home.

"It ain't changed," he said. "No use lookin' here." But he swung back the door and rummaged through books and papers, disturbing a chronometer and a small cash-box that held the schooner's limited amount of ready cash. There was no sign of any cartridges.

"We'll tackle Carlsen's room next," he announced. "I don't suppose you looked between the bunk mattresses, did you?"

"I never thought of it," said Rainey. "I didn't imagine there would be more than one."

"I've got a hunch you'll find two on Carlsen's bunk. An' the shells between 'em. He kep' his door locked when he was out of the main cabin an' slep' on 'em nights. That's what I'd be apt to do."

As they came into the main cabin Rainey caught Lund by the arm.

"I'm almost sure I saw Carlsen's door closing," he whispered. "It might have been the shadow."

"But it might not. Shouldn't wonder. One of 'em's sneaked in. Saw the cabin empty, an' figgered we'd turned in. While we was in the strong-room."

He took the automatic from his pocket and went straight to the door of Carlsen's room. It was locked or bolted from within.

"The fool!" said Lund. "I've got a good mind to let him stay there till he swallers some o' the drugs to fill his belly." He rapped on the panel with the butt of the gun.

"Come on out before I start trouble."

There was no answer. Lund looked uncertainly at Rainey.

"I hate to start a rumpus ag'in," he said, jerking his head toward the skipper's room. "'Count of her. Reckon he can stay there till after we've buried Simms. He's safe enough."

Rainey was a little surprised at this show of thoughtfulness, but he did not remark on it. He was beginning to think pretty constantly of late that he had underestimated Lund.

The giant's hand dropped automatically to the handle as if to assure himself of the door being fast. Suddenly it opened wide, a black gap, with only the gray eye of the porthole facing them. Lund had brought up the muzzle of his pistol to the height of a man's chest, but there was nothing to oppose it.

"Hidin', the damn fool! What kind of a game is this? Come out o' there."

Something scuttled on the floor of the room — then darted swiftly out between the legs of Lund and Rainey, on all fours, like a great dog. Curlike, it sprawled on the floor with a white face and pop-eyes, with hands outstretched in pleading, knees drawn up in some ludicrous attempt at protection, calling shrilly, in the voice of Sandy:

"Don't shoot, sir! Please don't shoot!"

Lund reached down and jerked the roustabout to his feet, half strangling him with his grip on the collar of the lad's shirt, and flung him into a chair.

"What were you doin' in there?"

Sandy gulped convulsively, feeling at his scraggy throat, where an Adam's apple was working up and down. Speech was scared out of him, and he could only roll his eyes at them.

"You damned young traitor!" said Lund. "I'll have you keelhauled for this! Out with it, now. Who sent ye? Deming?"

"You've got him frightened half to death," intervened Rainey. "They probably scared him into doing this. Didn't they, Sandy?"

The lad blinked, and tears of self-pity rolled down his grimy cheeks. The relief of them seemed to unstopper his voice. That, and the kinder quality of Rainey's questioning.

"Deming! He said he'd cut my bloody heart out if I didn't do it. Him an' Beale. Lookit."

He plucked aside the front of his almost buttonless shirt and worn undervest and showed them on his left breast the scoring where a sharp blade had marked an irregular circle on his skin.

"Beale did that," he whined. "Deming said they'd finish the job if I come back without 'em."

"Without the shells?"

"Yes, sir. Yes, Mr. Rainey. Oh, Gord, they'll kill me sure! Oh, my Gord!" His staring eyes and loose mouth, working in fear, made him look like a fresh-landed cod.

"You ain't much use alive," said Lund.

"Mebbe I ain't," returned the lad, with the desperation of a cornered rat. "But I got a right to live. And I've lived worse'n a dorg on this bloody schooner. I'm fair striped an' bruised wi' boots an' knuckles an' ends o' rope. I'd 'ave chucked myself over long ago if — "

"If what?"

The lad turned sullen.

"Never mind," he said, and glared almost defiantly at Lund.

"Is that door shut?" the giant asked Rainey. "Some of 'em might be hangin' 'round." Rainey went to the corridor and closed and locked the entrance.

"Now then, you young devil," said Lund. "What they did to you for'ard ain't a marker on what I'll do to you if you don't speak up an' answer when I talk. *If what?*"

Sandy turned to Rainey.

"They said they was goin' to give me some of the gold," he said. "They said all along I was to have the hat go 'round for me. I told you I was dragged up, but there's — there's an old woman who was good to me. She's up ag'in' it for fair. I told her I'd bring her back some dough an' if I can hang on an' git it, I'll hang on. But they'll do me up, now, for keeps."

Rainey heard Lund's chuckle ripen to a quiet laugh.

"I'm damned if they ain't some guts to the herrin' after all," he said. "Hangin' on to take some dough back to an old woman who ain't even his mother. Who'd have thought it? Look here, my lad. I was dragged up the same way, I was. An' I hung on. But you'll never git a cent out of that bunch. I don't know as they'll have enny to give you."

His face hardened. "But you come through, an' I'll see you git somethin' for the old woman. An' yoreself, too. What's more, you can stay aft an' wait on cabin. If they lay a finger on you, I'll lay a fist on them, an' worse."

"You ain't kiddin' me?"

"I don't kid, my lad. I don't waste time that way."

Sandy stood up, his face lighting. He began to empty his pockets, laying shells and shotgun cartridges upon the table.

"I couldn't begin to git harf of 'em," he said. "The rest's under the mattresses. They said they on'y needed a few. I thought you was both turned in. When you come out of the corridor I was scared nutty."

Between the mattresses, as Lund had guessed, they found the rest of the shells, laid out in orderly rows save where the lad's scrambling fingers had disturbed them. Lund stripped off a pillow-case and dumped them in, together with those on the table.

"You can bunk here," he told the grateful Sandy. "Now I'll have a few words with Deming, Beale and Company. Want to come along, Rainey?"

Lund strode down the corridor, bag in one hand, his gun in the other. Rainey threw open the door of the hunters' quarters and discovered them like a lot of conspirators. Deming was in his bunk; also another man, whose ribs Lund had cracked when he had kicked him along the deck out of his way. The bruised faces of the rest showed their effects from the fight. As Lund entered, covering them with the gun, while he swung down the heavy slip on the table with a clatter, their looks changed from eager expectation to consternation.

CHAPTER XIV
PEGGY SIMMS

"Caught with the goods!" said Lund. "Two tries at mutiny in one day, my lads. You want to git it into your boneheads that I'm runnin' this ship from now on. I can sail it without ye and, by God, I'll set the bunch of ye ashore same's you figgered on doin' with me if you don't sit up an' take notice! The rifles an' guns" — he glanced at the orderly display of weapons in racks on the wall — "are too vallyble to chuck over, but here go the shells, ev'ry last one of them. So that nips *that* little plan, Deming."

He turned back the slip to display the contents.

"Open a port, Rainey, an' heave the lot out."

Rainey did so while the hunters gazed on in silent chagrin.

"There's one thing more," said Lund, grinning at them. "If enny of you saw a man hurtin' a dog, you'd probably fetch him a wallop. But you don't think ennything of scarin' the life out of a half-baked kid an' markin' up his hide like a patchwork quilt. Thet kid's stayin' aft after this. One of you monkey with him, an' you'll do jest what he's bin doin', wish you was dead an' overboard."

He turned on his heel and walked to the door, Rainey following.

"Burial of the skipper at dawn," said Lund. "All hands on deck, clean an' neatly dressed to stand by. An' see yore behavior fits the occasion. Deming, you'll turn out, too. No malingerin'."

It was plain that the news of the captain's death was known to them. They showed no surprise. Rainey was sure that Tamada had not mentioned it. It had leaked out through the grape-vine telegraphy of all ships. Doubtless, he thought, the after-cabin and its doings was always being spied upon.

"Will you take the service ter-morrer?" Lund asked Rainey when they were back in the cabin. "Bein' as yo're an eddicated chap?"

"Why — I don't know it. Is there a prayer-book aboard? I thought the skipper always presided."

"I'm only deputy-skipper w'en it comes down to that," said Lund. "It ain't my ship. I'm jest runnin' it under contract with my late partner. The ship belongs to the gal. And yo're top officer now, in the regular run. As to a prayer-book, there ain't sech an article aboard to my knowledge. But I'd like to have it go off shipshape. For Simms' sake as well as the gal's. I reckon he used his best jedgment 'bout puttin' back after me on the floe. I might have done the same thing myself."

Rainey doubted that statement, and set it down to Lund's generosity. Many of his late words and actions had displayed a latent depth of feeling that he had never credited Lund with possessing. He could not help believing that, in some way, the girl had brought them to the surface.

"I thought I saw a Bible in the safe," he said, "when we were looking for the shells. There may be a prayer-book. I suppose there have been occasions for it. The mate died at sea last trip."

"There may be," returned Lund. "That's where Simms 'ud keep it. He warn't what you'd call a religious man. We'll take a look afore we turn in."

There were offices to be performed for the dead captain that the girl, with all her willingness, could not attempt. Lund did not mention them, and Rainey vacillated about disturbing her until he saw Tamada go through the cabin with folded canvas and a flag. The Japanese tapped on the door, which was instantly opened to him. He had been expected.

There was no doubt that Tamada, with his medical experience, was best fitted for the task, but it seemed to Rainey also that the girl had deliberately ignored their services and that, despite her involuntary admiration of Lund's fight against odds, or in revulsion of it, she reckoned them hostile to her sentiments. Lund roused him by talking of the burial-service for Simms.

"You're a writer," he said. "What's the good of knowin' how to handle words if you can't fake up some sort of a service? One's as good as another, long as it sounds like the real thing.

"I reckon there's a God," he went on. "Somethin' that started things, somethin' that keeps the stars from runnin' each other down, but, after He wound up the clock He made, I don't figger He bothers much about the works.

"Luck's the big thing that counts. We're all in on the deal. Some of us git the deuces an' treys, an' some git the aces. If yo're born lucky things go soft for you. But, if it warn't for luck, for the chance an' the hope of it, things 'ud be upside down an' plain anarchy in a jiffy. If it warn't the pore devil's idea that his luck has got to change for the better, mebbe ter-morrer, he'd start out an' cut his own throat, or some one else's, if he had ginger enough."

"It's hardly all luck, is it?" asked Rainey. "Look at you! You're bigger than most men, stronger, better equipped to get what you want."

"Hell!" laughed Lund. "I was lucky to be born that way. But you've got to fudge up some sort of a service to suit the gal. You've got that Bible. It ought to be easy. Simms wouldn't give a whoop, enny more'n I would. When yo're dead yo're through, so far's enny one can prove it to you. A dead body's a nuisance, an' the sooner it's got rid of the better. But if it's goin' to make the livin' feel enny better for spielin' off some fine words, why, hop to it an' make up yore speech."

Peggy Simms saved Rainey by producing a prayer-book, bringing it to Lund, her face pale but composed enough, and her shadowed eyes calm as she gave it to him.

"I reckon Rainey here 'ud read it better'n me," he said. "He's a scholar."

"If you will," asked the girl. She seemed to have outworn her first sorrow, to have obtained a grip of herself that, with the dignity of her bereavement, the very control of her undoubted grief, set up a barrier between her and Lund. Rainey was conscious of this fence behind which the girl had retreated. She was polite, but she did not ask this service as a favor, as a friendly act. Refusal, even, would not have visibly affected her, he fancied. There was an invisible armor about her that might be added to at any moment by a shield of silent scorn. Somehow, if sex had, for a swift moment, brought her and Lund into any contact, that same sex, showing another aspect, set them far apart.

Lund showed that he felt it, running his splay fingers through his beard in evident embarrassment, while Rainey took the book silently, looking through the pages for the ritual of "Burial at Sea."

Arrangements had been made on deck long before dawn. A section of the rail had been removed and a grating arranged that could be tipped at the right moment for the consignment of the captain's body to the deep.

The sea was running in long heaves, and the sun rose in a clear sky. The ocean was free from ice, though the wind was cold. Here and there a berg, far off, caught the sparkle of the sun and, to the north, parallel to their course, the peaks of the Aleutian Isles, broken buttresses of an ancient seabridge, showed sharply against the horizon.

At four bells in the morning watch all hands had assembled, save for Tamada and Hansen, who appeared bearing the canvas-enveloped, flag-draped body of Simms, his sea-shroud weighted by heavy pieces of iron. Peggy Simms followed them, and, as the crew, with shuffling feet and throats that were repeatedly cleared, gathered in a semicircle, she arranged the folds of the Stars and Stripes that Hansen attached to a light line by one corner.

Whatever Lund affected, the solemnity of the occasion held the men. They uncovered and stood with bowed heads that hid the bruised faces of the hunters. Lund's own damaged features were lowered as Rainey commenced to read. Only Deming's face, gray from the effort of coming on deck and the pain in his arm, held the semblance of a sneer that was largely bravado. A hunter had his arm tucked in that of his comrade with the broken ribs. A seaman was told off to the wheel and the schooner was held to the wind with all sheets close inboard, rising and falling on an almost level keel.

"And the body shall be cast into the sea."

At the words Lund and Hansen tilted the grating. There was a slight pause as if the body were reluctant to start on its last journey, and then it slid from the platform and plunged into the sea, disappearing instantly under the urge of the weights, with a hissing aeration of the water. The flag, held inboard by the line, fluttered a moment and subsided over the grating. The girl turned toward them, her head up.

"Thank you," she said, and went below.

"That's over," said Lund, letting out whatever emotions he might have repressed in a long breath. "Now, then, trim ship! Watch-off, get below. We're goin' to drive her for all she's worth."

He took the wheel himself as the men jumped to the sheets and soon Lund was getting every foot of possible speed out of the schooner. He was as good a sailor as Simms, inclined to take more chances, but capable of handling them.

The girl kept below and seldom came out of her cabin, Tamada serving her meals in there. Rainey could see Lund's resentment growing at this attitude that seemed to him normal enough, though it might present difficulty later if persisted in. But the morning that they headed up through Sequam Pass between the spouting reefs of Sequam and Amlia Islands, she came on deck and went forward to the bows, taking in deep breaths of the bracing air and gazing north to the free expanse of Bering Strait. Rainey left her alone, but Lund welcomed her as she came back aft.

"Glad to see you on deck again, Miss Peggy," he said. "You need sun and air to git you in shape again."

His glance held vivid admiration of her as he spoke, a glance that ran over her rounded figure with a frank approval that Rainey resented, but to which the girl paid no attention. She seemed to have made up her mind to a change of attitude.

"How far have we yet to go?" she asked.

"A'most a thousan' miles to the Strait proper," said Lund. "The Nome-Unalaska steamer lane lies to the east. Runs close to the Pribilofs, three hundred miles north, with Hall an' St. Matthew three hundred further. Then comes St. Lawrence Isle, plumb in the middle of the Strait, with Siberia an' Alaska closin' in."

He was keen to hold her in conversation, and she willing to listen, assenting almost eagerly when he offered to point out their positions on the chart, spread on the cabin table. Lund talked well, for all his limited and at times luridly inclined vocabulary, whenever he talked of the sea and of his own adventures, stating them without brag, but bringing up striking pictures of action, full of the color and savor of life in the raw. From that time on Peggy Simms came to the table and talked freely with Lund, more conservatively with Rainey.

The newspaperman was no experienced analyst of woman nature, but he saw, or thought he saw, the girl watching Lund closely when he talked, studying him, sometimes with more than a hint of approbation, at others with a look that was puzzled, seeming to be working at a problem. The giant's liking for her, boyish at times, or swiftly changing to bolder appraisal, grew daily.

The girl, Rainey decided, was humoring Lund, seeking to know how with her feminine methods she might control him, keep him within bounds. Her coldness, it seemed, she had cast aside as an expedient that might prove too provoking and worthless.

And Rainey's valuation of her resources increased. She was handling her woman's weapons admirably, yet when he sometimes, at night, under the cabin lamp, saw the smoldering light glowing in Lund's agate eyes, he knew that she was playing a dangerous game.

"What d'ye figger on doin' with yore share, Rainey?" Lund asked him the night that they passed Nome. It was stormy weather in the Strait, and the *Karluk* was snugged down under treble reefs, fighting her way north. Ice in the Narrows was scarce, though Lund predicted broken floes once they got through. The cabin was cozy, with a stove going. Peggy Simms was busied with some sewing, the canary and the plants gave the place a domestic atmosphere, and Lund, smoking comfortably, was eminently at ease.

"'Cordin' to the way the men figgered it out," he went on, "though I reckon they're under the mark more'n over it, you'll have forty thousan' dollars. That's quite a windfall, though nothin' to Miss Peggy, here, or me, for that matter. I s'pose you got it all spent already."

"I don't know that I have," said Rainey. "But I think, if all goes well, I'll get a place up in the Coast Range, in the redwoods looking over the sea, and write. Not newspaper stuff, but what I've always wanted to. Stories. Yarns of adventure!"

Peggy Simms looked up.

"You've never done that?" she asked.

"Not satisfactorily. I suppose that genius burns in a garret, but I don't imagine myself a genius and I don't like garrets. I've an idea I can write better when I don't have to stand the bread-and-butter strain of routine."

"Goin' to write second-hand stuff?" asked Lund. "Why don't you *live* what you write? I don't see how yo're goin' to git under a man's skin by squattin' in a bungalow with a Jap servant, a porcelain bathtub, an' breakfast in bed. Why don't you travel an' see stuff as it is? How in blazes are you goin' to write Adventure if you don't live it?

"Me, I'm goin' to git a schooner built accordin' to my own ideas. Have a kicker engine in it, mebbe, an' go round the world. What's the use of livin' on it an' not knowin' it by sight? Books and pictures are all right in their way, I reckon, but, while my riggin' holds up, I'm for travel. Mebbe I'll take a group of islands down in the South Seas after a bit an' make somethin' out of 'em. Not jest *copra* an' pearl-shell, but cotton an' rubber."

"A king and his kingdom," suggested the girl.

"Aye, an' mebbe a queen to go with it," replied Lund, his eyes wide open in a look that made the girl flush and Rainey feel the hidden issue that he felt was bound to come, rising to the surface.

"That's a *man's* life," went on Lund. "Travel's all right, but a man's got to do somethin', buck somethin', start somethin'. An' a red-blooded man wants the right kind of a woman to play mate. Polish off his rough edges, mebbe. I'd rather be a rough castin' that could stand filin' a bit, than smooth an' plated. An', when I find the right woman, one of my own breed, I'm goin' to tie to her an' her to me.

"I'm goin' to be rich. They've cleaned up the sands of Nome, but there's others'll be found yit between Cape Hope an' Cape Barry. Meantime, we've got a placer of our own. With plenty of gold they ain't much limit to what a man can do. I've roughed it all my life, an' I'm not lookin' for ease. It makes a man soft. But —"

He swept the figure of the girl in a pause that was eloquent of his line of thought. She grew uneasy of it, but Lund maintained it until she raised her eyes from her work and challenged his. Rainey saw her breast heave, saw her struggle to hold the gaze, turn red, then pale. He thought her eyes showed fear, and then she stiffened. Almost unconsciously she raised her hand to where Rainey was sure she kept the little pistol, touched something as though to assure herself of its presence, and went on sewing. Lund chuckled, but shifted his eyes to Rainey.

"Why don't you write up *this* v'yage? When it's all over? There's adventure for you, an' we ain't ha'f through with it. An' romance, too, mebbe. We ain't developed much of a love-story as yit, but you never can tell."

He laughed, and Peggy Simms got up quietly, folded her sewing, and said "Good night" composedly before she went to her room.

"How about it, Rainey?" quizzed Lund. "How about the love part of it? She's a beauty, an' she'll be an heiress. Ain't you got enny red blood in yore veins? Don't you want her? You won't find many to hold a candle to her. Looks, built like a racin' yacht, smooth an' speedy. Smart, an' rich into the bargain. Why don't you make love to her?"

Rainey felt the burning blood mounting to his face and brain.

"I am not in love with Miss Simms," he said. "If I was I should not try to make love to her under the circumstances. She's alone, and she's fatherless. I do not care to discuss her."

"She's a woman," said Lund. "And yo're a damned prig! You'd like to bust me in the jaw, but you know I'm stronger. You've got some guts, Rainey, but yo're hidebound. You ain't got ha'f the git-up-an'-go to ye that she has. She's a woman, I tell you, an' she's to be won. If you want her, why don't you stand up an' try to git her 'stead of sittin' around like a sick cat whenever I happen to admire her looks?

"I've seen you. I ain't blind enny longer, you know. She's a woman an' I'm a man. I thought you was one. But you ain't. Yore idea of makin' love is to send the gal a box of candy an' walk pussy-footed an' write poems to her. You want to *write* life an' I want to *live* it. So does a gal like that. She's more my breed than yores, if she has got eddication. An' she's flesh and blood. Same as I am. Yo're half sawdust. Yo're stuffed."

He went on deck laughing, leaving Rainey raging but helpless. Lund appeared to think the situation obvious. Two men, and a woman who was attractive in many ways. The *only* woman while they were aboard the schooner, therefore the more to be desired, admired by men cut off from the rest of the world.

He expected Rainey to be in love with her, to stand up and say so, to endeavor to win her. Lund sought the ardor of competition. He might be looking for the excuse to crush Rainey.

But he had said she was of his breed, and that was a true saying. If Lund was a son of the sea, she was a daughter of a line of seamen. Lund, sooner or later, meant to take her, willing or unwilling. He had said so, none too covertly, that very evening. And, if Rainey meant to stand between her and Lund as a protector, Lund would accept him in that character only as the girl's lover and his rival.

And Rainey did not know whether he was in love with her or not. He could not even be certain of the girl. There were times when Lund seemed to fascinate her. One thing he braced himself to do, to be ready to aid her against Lund if occasion came, and she needed protection. The luck, as Lund phrased it, that had given brawn to the giant, had given Rainey brains. When the time came he would use them.

After this the girl avoided Lund's company as much as possible by seeking Rainey's. They worked through the Strait and headed into the Arctic Ocean. Ice was all about them, fields formed of vast blocks of frozen water divided by broad lanes through which the *Karluk* slowly made her way, a maze of ice, always threatening, calling for all of Lund's skill while he fumed at every barrier, every change of the weather that grew steadily colder.

The sky was never entirely unveiled by mist, and at night, as they sailed down a frozen fiord with lookouts doubled, the grinding smashing noises of the ice seemed the warning voice of the North, as they sailed on into the wilderness.

The hunters kept below. Lund bossed the ship. Deming, it seemed, managed to hold his cards and deal them despite his mending arm in splints. And he was steadily winning. The girl talked with Rainey of her own life ashore and at sea on earlier trips with her father, of his own desire to write, of his ambitions, until there was little he had not told her, even to the girl who was the daughter of the Lumber King.

And the spell of her nearness, her youth, her beauty, naturally held him. When he was on deck duty she remained in her room. When Lund relieved him, the day's work giving Lund, Hansen, and Rainey each two regular watches of four hours, though Lund put in most of the night as the ice grew more difficult to navigate, Rainey occasionally saw the giant's eyes sizing him up with a sardonic twinkle.

For the time being, the safety of the *Karluk* and the successful carrying out of the purpose of the trip took all of Lund's attention and energy. Twice he had been thwarted by the weather from gleaning his golden harvest, and it began to look as if the third attempt might be no more fortunate.

"The *Karluk's* stout," he said once, "but she ain't built for the Arctic. If we git nipped badly she'll go like an eggshell."

"And then what?" Rainey asked.

"Git the gold! That's what we come for. If we have to make sleds an' use the hunters for a dorg-team." He laughed indomitably. "We'll make a man of you yit, Rainey, afore we git back."

Lund was snatching sleep in scraps, seeking always to feel a way toward the position of the island through the ice that continually baffled progress. Several times they risked the schooner in a narrow lane when a lull of the often uncertain wind would have seen them ground between the edges of the floe. Twice Lund ordered out the boats to save them. Once all hands fended desperately with spars to keep her clear, and only the schooner's overhung stern saved her rudder from the savagely clashing masses that closed behind them.

But he showed few signs of strain. Once in a while he would sit with closed eyes or pass his hands across his brows as if they pained him. But he never complained, and the ice, taking on the dull hues of sea and sky, gave off no glare that should affect the sight. Against all opposition Lund forced his way until, just after sunset one night, as the dusk swept down, he gave a shout and pointed to a fitful flare over the port bow. Rainey thought it the aurora, but Lund laughed at him.

"It's the crater atop the island," he said. "Nothin' dangerous. Reg'lar lighthouse. Now, boys," he went on, his deep voice ringing with exhilaration, "there's gold in sight! Whistle for a change of weather, every mother's son of you!"

The deck was soon crowded. On the previous trip the schooner had approached the island from a different angle, but the men were swift to acknowledge the glow of the volcano as the expected landfall. Lund remained on deck, and it was late before any of the crew turned in. Rainey, during his watch, saw the mountain fire-pulse, glowing and winking like the eye of a Cyclops, its gleam reflected in the eyes of the watchers who were about to invade the island and rob it of its golden sands.

The change of weather came about three in the morning, though not as Lund had hoped. A sudden wind materialized from the north, stiffening the canvas with its ice-laden breath, glazing the schooner wherever moisture dripped, bringing up an angry scud of clouds that fought with the moon. The sea appeared to have thickened. The *Karluk* went sluggishly, as if she was sailing in a sea of treacle.

"Half slush already," said Lund. "We're in for a real cold snap. There'll be pancake ice all around us afore dawn. That is sure a hard beach to fetch. But it's too early for winter closing. After this nip we'll have a warm spell. An' we got to git the stuff aboard an' start kitin' south afore the big freeze-up catches us."

When Rainey came on deck the next morning he found the schooner floating in a small lagoon that made the center of a floe. The water in it was slush, half solid. Main and fore were close furled, the headsails also, and the *Karluk* was nosing against the far end of the rapidly diminishing basin. The wind was still lively.

All about were other floes, but they were widely separated, and between them crisp waves of indigo were curling snappily.

The island stood up sharp and jagged, much larger than Rainey had anticipated. It boasted two cones, from one of which smoke was lazily trailing. Ice was piled in wild confusion about its shores, wrecked by the gale that had blown hard from four till eight, and was now subsiding with the swift change common to the Arctic.

A deep hum of bursting surf undertoned all other noises and, prisoned as she was, the schooner and her floe were sweeping slowly toward the land in the grip of a current rather than before the gusty wind.

Lund had fendered the schooner's bows effectively before he went below with old sails that enveloped stem and swell, stuffed with ropes and bits of canvas.

Within an hour the wind had ceased and the slush in the lagoon had pancaked into flakes of forming ice that bid fair to become solid within a short time, for the day was bitterly cold and tremendously bright. The sky rose from filmy silver-azure to richest sapphire, and the rolling waters between the floes were darkest purple-blue. As the whip of the wind ceased they settled to a vast swell on which the great clumps of ice rose and fell with dazzling reflections.

Lund came up within the hour and stood blinking at the brilliance.

"My eyes ain't as strong yit as they should be," he said to Rainey. "I shouldn't have slung them glasses so hasty at Carlsen, though they sp'iled his aim, at that. If this weather keeps up I'll have to make snow-specs; there ain't another pair of smokes aboard." He made a shade of his curved hand as he gazed at the island.

"Current's got us," he said, "an' we'll fetch up mighty close to the beach. It lies between those two ridges, close together, buttin' out from the volcano. Long Strait current splits on Wrangell Island, and we're in the trend of the northern loop. That's why the sea don't freeze up more solid. It's freezin' fast enough round us, where there ain't motion."

He seemed well satisfied with the prospect. "Had breakfast?" he asked Rainey, and then: "All right. We'll git the men aft."

He bellowed an order, and soon every one came trooping, to gather in two groups either side of the cabin skylight. Their faces were eager with the proximity of the gold, yet half sullen as they waited to hear what Lund had to say. Since the attempt against him Lund had said nothing about their shares. They acknowledged him as master, but they still rebelled in spirit.

"There's the island," said Lund. "We'll make it afore sundown. The beach is there, waitin' for us to dig it up. It'll be some job. I don't reckon it's frozen hard, on'y crusted. If it is we'll bust the crust with dynamite. But we got to hop to it. There'll be another cold spell after this one peters out an' the next is like to be permanent. I want the gold washed out afore then, an' us well down the Strait. It's up to you to hump yoreselves, an' I'll help the humpin'.

"We'll cradle most of the stuff an', if they's time, we'll flume the silt tailin's for the fine dust. Providin' we can git a fall of water. There'll be plenty for all hands to do. An' the shares go as first fixed. I ain't expectin' you to do the diggin' an' not git a pinch or two of the dust."

The men's faces lighted, and they shuffled about, looking at one another with grins of relief.

"No cheers?" asked Lund ironically. "Wall, I hardly expected enny. Hansen, you'll be one of the foremen, with pay accordin'. Deming."

"I can't dig," said the hunter truculently. "Neither can Beale, with his ribs."

"You've got a sweet nerve," said Lund. "I reckon you've won enough to be sure of yore shares, if the boys pay up. Enough for you to do some diggin' in yore pockets for Beale. His ribs 'ud be whole if you hadn't started the bolshevik stunt. But I'll find something for both of you to do. Don't let that worry you none.

"We've got mercury aboard somewhere," Lund continued, to Rainey, when the men had dispersed, far more cheerful than they had gathered. "We'll use that for concentration in the film riffles. Hansen'll have rockers made that'll catch the big stuff. If the worst comes to the worst, we'll load up the old hooker with the pay dirt an' wash it out on the way home. I'll strip that beach down to bedrock if I have to work the toes an' fingers off 'em."

By noon the schooner was glazed in as firmly as a toy model that is mounted in a glass sea. The wind blew itself entirely out, but the current bore them steadily on to the clamorous shore, where the swells were creating promontories, bays, cliffs and chasms in the piled-up confusion of the floes pounding on the rocks, breaking up or sliding atop one another in noisy confusion.

The marble-whiteness of the ice masses was set off by the blues and soft violets of their shadows, and by a pearly sheen wherever the planes caught the light at a proper slant for the play of prisms. Beautiful as it was, the sight was fearful to Rainey, in common with the crew. Only Lund surveyed it nonchalantly.

"It's bustin' up fast," he said. "All we need is a little luck. If we ain't got that there's no use of worryin'. We can't blast ourselves out o' this without riskin' the schooner. We ought to be thankful we froze in gentle. There ain't a plank started. The floe'll fend us off. There ain't enny big chunks enny way near us aft. Luck — to make a decent landin' — is all we need, an' it's my hunch it's comin' our way."

His "hunch" was correct. Though they did not actually make the little bay on which the treasure beach debouched, they fetched up near it against a broken hill of ice that had lodged on the sharp slopes of a little promontory, making the connection without further damage than a splitting of the forward end of their encasing floe, with hardly a jar to the *Karluk*.

Lund sent men ashore over the ice, climbing to the promontory crags with hawsers by which they tied up schooner, floe and all, to the land. If the broken hill suffered further catastrophe, which did not seem likely, its fragments would fall upon the floe. In case of emergency Lund ordered men told off day and night to stand by the hawsers, to cast loose or cut, as the extremity needed.

The main danger threatened from following floes piling up on theirs and ramming over it to smash the schooner, but that was a risk that must be met as it evolved, and there did not seem much prospect of the happening.

It was dark before they were snugged. The men volunteered, through Hansen, to commence digging that night by the light of big fires, so crazy were they at the nearness of the gold. But Lund forbade it.

"You'll work reg'lar shifts when you git started," he said. "An' you won't start till ter-morrer. We've got to stand by the ship ter-night until we find out by mornin' how snug we're goin' to be berthed."

All night long they lay in a pandemonium of noise. After a while they would become used to it as do the workers in a stampmill, but that night it deafened them, kept them awake and alert, fearful, with the tremendous cannonading. The bite of the frost made the timbers of the *Karluk* creak and its thrust continually worked among the stranded masses with groaning thunders and shrill grindings, while the surf ever boomed on the resonant sheets of ice.

The place held a strange mystery. On top of the main cone the volcanic glow hung above the crater chimney, reflected waveringly on the rolling clouds of smoke that blotted out the stars. There were no tremors, no rumblings from the hidden furnace, only the flare of its stoking. The stars that were visible were intensely brilliant points, and, when the moon rose, it was accompanied by four mock moons bound in a halo that widely encircled the true orb. The moon-dogs shone intermittently with prismatic colors, like disks of mother-of-pearl, and the moon itself was four-rayed.

Under moon and stars the coast snaked away to end in a deceptive glimmer that persisted beyond the eye-range of definite dimensions. And, despite all the sound, muffled and sharp, of splinterings and explosions, of the reverberation of the swell, outside all this clamor, silence seemed to gather and to wait. Silence and loneliness. It awed the crew, it invested the spirits of Peggy Simms and Rainey, gazing at the mystic beauty of the Arctic landscape.

The walls of forced-up ice shifted about them and came clattering down, booming on their floe as if it had been a drum, and threatening to tilt it by sheer weight had they not been fairly grounded forward. Other floes came from seaward to batter at the cliffs, but the eddy that had brought them to their resting-place seemed to have been dissolved in the main current and, save for an occasional alarm, their stern was not seriously invaded.

Only, as the night wore on, the floating masses became cemented to one another and the shore. The *Karluk* was hard and fast within two hundred yards of her Tom Tiddler's ground, just over the promontory. If a thaw came, all should go well. If Lund had been deceived, and the true winter was setting in early, the prospects were far from cheerful, though no one seemed to think of that possibility.

Beneath the glamour of the magic night, the weird paraselene of the moon's phenomenon, the glow of the volcano, the noises, the men whispered of one thing only — Gold!

Dawn came before they were aware of it, a sudden rush of light that dyed the ice in every hue of red and orange, that tipped the frozen coast with bursts of ruby flame that flared like beacons and gilded the crests of the long swells, tinging all their world with a wild, unnatural glory.

Lund, striding the deck, his red beard iced with his breath, suddenly stopped and stared into the east. There, in the very eye of the dawn, was a trail of smoke, like a plume against the flaming, three-quarters circle of the rising sun!

CHAPTER XVI

THE MIGHT OF NIPPON

Lund's face, on which the bruises were fast fading, changed purple-black with rage. He whirled upon Sandy, gaping near, and ordered him to fetch his binoculars. Through them he stared long at the smoke. Then he turned to the girl and Rainey.

"Come down inter the cabin," he said. "We'll need all our wits."

"That's a gunboat patrol," he said. "Japanese, for a million! None other this far west. An' it's damned funny it should come up right at this minnit. We've made the trip on schedule time, an' here they show. But we'll let that slide. We've got to think fast. They'll board us. They'll overhaul us lookin' for seal pelts. At least, I hope so.

"We've got none. Our hunters an' our rifles an' shotguns'll prove our claim to be pelagic sealers. We got to trust they believe us. If there was a hide aboard or a club, or a sign of a dead seal on the beaches they'd nail us. They may, ennyway, jest on suspicion.

"They run things out this way with a high hand. If they ever clap us in prison it'll be where we can't let a peep out of us. A lot they worry about our consuls. They's too many good sealers dropped out of sight in one of their stinkin' jails to starve on millet an' dried, moldy fish. I know what I'm talkin' about.

"It's lucky we didn't start mussin' up that beach. But they'll go over everything. I know 'em. They claim to own the seas hereabouts, an' they're cockier than ever, since the war. Rainey you got to git busy on the log. If yore father didn't keep it up, Miss Peggy, so much the better. If he has, you got to fake it someways, Rainey.

"I'm Simms, get me, until we're clear of 'em. An' you, Rainey, are Doc Carlsen. Nothin' must show in the log about enny deaths."

"But why?" asked the girl. "Why do we have to masquerade? If we haven't touched the seals?"

Lund barked at her:

"I gave you credit for sharper wits," he said. "We've got to have everything so reg'lar they can't find an excuse for haulin' us in an' settin' fire to the schooner. They'd do it in a jiffy. We got to show 'em our clearance papers, an' we've got to tally up all down the line. Rainey ain't on the ship's books — Carlsen is. Lund ain't, but Simms is. I'm Simms. An' you" — he stopped to grin at her — "you're my daughter. I'll dissolve the relationship after a while, I'll promise you that. An' I'll drill the men. They know what's ahead of 'em if the Japs git suspicious.

"That ain't the worst of it! *They may know what we're after.* If they do, we're goners. Ever occur to you, Rainey, that Tamada, who is a deep one, may have tipped off the whole thing to his consul while the schooner was at San Francisco? He was along the last trip. He'd know the approximate position. Might have got the right figgers out o' the log, him havin' the run of the cabin. A cable would do the rest. He'd git his whack out of it, with the order of the Golden Chrysanthemum or some jig-arig to boot, an' git even with the way he feels to'ard our outfit for'ard, that ain't bin none too sweet to him."

The suggestion held a foundation of conviction for Rainey. He had thought of the consul. He had always sensed depths in Tamada's reserve, he remembered bits of his talk, the "certain circumstances" that he had mentioned. It looked plausible. Lund rose.

"I'll fix Tamada," he said. But the girl stopped him.

"You don't *know* that's true. Tamada has been wonderful — to me. What do you intend to do with him?"

"I'll make up my mind between here and the galley," said Lund grimly. "This is my third time of tackling this island, an' no Jap is goin' to stand between me an' the gold, this trip. Why, even if he ain't blown on us, he'll give the whole thing away. If he didn't want to they'd make him come through if they laid their eyes on him. They've got more tricks than a Chinese mandarin to make a man talk. Stands to reason he'll tell 'em. If he can talk when they git here," he added ominously, standing half-way between the table and the door to the corridor, his hand opening and closing suggestively. "The crew'd settle his hash if I didn't. They ain't fools. They know what's ahead of 'em in Japan. You, Rainey, git busy with that log. That gunboat'll have a boat alongside this floe inside of ninety minnits."

But Peggy Simms was between him and the door.

"You shan't do it," she said, her eyes hard as flints, if Lund's were like steel. "You don't know what he was to me when — when dad was buried. Call him in and let him talk for himself or — or *I'll tell the Japanese myself what we have come for!*"

Lund stood staring at her, his face hard, his beard thrust out like a bush with the jut of his jaw. Still she faced him, resolute, barely up to his shoulder, slim, defiant. Gradually his features crinkled into a grin.

"I believe you would," he said at last. "An' I'd hate to fix you the way I would Tamada. But, mind you, if I don't git a definite promise out of him that rings true, I'll have to stow him somewheres, where they won't find him. An' that won't be on board ship."

The girl's face softened.

"You said you played fair," she said with a sigh of relief. She stepped to the door, opened it, and called for Tamada. The Japanese appeared almost instantly. Lund closed the door behind him and locked it.

"You know there's a patrol comin' up, Tamada?" he asked. "A Jap patrol?"

"Yes."

"What do you intend tellin' 'em if they come on board?"

"Nothing, if I can help it. I think I can. I am not friendly with Japanese government. It would be bad for me if they find me. One time I belong Progressive Party in Japan. I make much talk. Too much. The government say I am too progressive."

Rainey imagined he caught a glint of humor in Tamada's eyes as he made his clipped syllables.

"So, I leave my country. Suppose I go on steamer I think that government they stop me. I think even in California they may make trouble, if they find me. So I go in *sampan*. Sometimes Japanese cross to California in *sampan*."

"That's right," said Rainey. He had handled more than one story of Japanese crews landing on some desolate portion of the coast to avoid immigration laws and steamer fares. Generally they were rounded up after their perilous, daring crossing of the Pacific. Tamada's story held the elements of truth. Even Lund nodded in reserved affirmation.

"Also I ship on *Karluk* as cook because of perhaps trouble if some one know me in San Francisco. I think much better if they do not see me. I have a plan. Also I want my share of gold. Suppose that gunboat find me, find out about gold, they will not give me reward. You do not know Japanese. They will put me in prison. It will be suggest to me, because I am of *daimio* blood" — Tamada drew himself up slightly as he claimed his nobility — "that I make *hari-kari*. That I do not wish. I am Progressive. I much rather cook on board *Karluk* and get my share of gold."

Lund surveyed him moodily, half convinced. The girl was all eager approval.

"What is your plan, Tamada?"

"We're losin' time on that log," cut in Lund. "Git busy, Rainey. Look among Carlsen's stuff. He may have kept one. Dope up one of 'em, an' burn the other. Now then, Tamada, dope out yore scheme; it's got to be a good one."

Both Lund and the girl were laughing when Rainey came out into the main cabin again with the records. Tamada had disappeared.

"He's some fox," said Lund. "Miss Peggy, you better superintend the theatricals. It's got to be done right. Rainey, not to interrupt you, what do you know about enteric fever?"

"Nothing."

"Well, it's the same as typhoid. There'll be a surgeon aboard that gunboat. You got to bluff him. Say little an' look wise as an' owl. Don't let him mix in with yore patient."

"My patient?"

"Tamada! He's got enteric fever. If there's time he'll give you all the dope."

"But I don't see how that — "

"You will see when you see Tamada," Lund grinned. "How about them logs? Can you fix 'em?"

"I think so."

"Then hop to it. I'm goin' to wise up the men and arrange a reception committee. Don't forgit yore name's Carlsen, an' mine's Simms."

Rainey wrote rapidly in his log, erasing, eliminating pages without trace, imitating the skipper's phrasing. Fortunately Simms had made scant entries at first and, later on, as the drug held him, none at all. Carlsen had kept no record that he could find. The girl had gone forward to aid with Tamada's plan which Lund had evidently accepted.

Before he had quite finished he heard the tramp of men on deck and the blast of a steam whistle. He ended his task and went up to see the gunboat, gray and menacing, its brasses glistening, men on her decks at their tasks, oblivious of the schooner, and officers on her bridge watching the progress of a launch toward the floe.

It made landing smartly, and a lieutenant, diminutive but highly effective in appearance, led six men toward the *Karluk*. He wore a sword and revolver; the men carried carbines. Their disciplined rank and smartness, the waiting launch, the gunboat in the offing, were ominous with the suggestion of power, the will to administer it. The officer in command carried his chin at an arrogant tilt. Lund had rigged a gangway and stood at the head of it, saluting the lieutenant as the latter snappily answered the greeting.

Rainey found the girl and put a hurried question.

"What about Tamada? Where is he? What's the plan?"

She turned to him with eyes that danced with excitement.

"He's in the galley, Doctor Carlsen. But he isn't Tamada any more. He's Jim Cuffee, nigger cook, sick with enteric fever, not to be disturbed."

Rainey stared. It was a clever device, if Tamada could carry it out, and he bear his own part in the masquerade. The willingness of Tamada to risk the disguise was assurance of his fidelity.

"Lund should have told me," he said. "I've got to change his name on the papers. It won't take a minute though; he doesn't appear in the log."

The Japanese officer wasted no time on deck. For precaution, Rainey made his alteration in the skipper's cabin, leaving the log there on the built-in desk.

"This is Lieutenant Ito, Doctor Carlsen," said Lund. "You want to see our papers, Lieutenant?"

"My orders are to examine the schooner," said Ito, in English, even more perfect than Tamada's. His face was officially severe, though his slant eyes shifted constantly toward the girl. Evidently she was an unexpected feature of the visit.

"I'll get the papers first," said Lund. "Doctor, you an' Peggy entertain the lieutenant." Rainey set out some whisky, which the Japanese refused, some cigars that he passed over with a motion of his hand. He sat down stiffly and ran through the papers.

"We're pelagic, you know," said Lund. "We ain't trespassin' on purpose. Didn't even know you owned the island."

"It is on our charts," said Ito crisply, as if that settled the right of dominion. "How did you come here at all?"

"We was brought," said Lund. "Got froze in north o' Wrangell. Gale set us west as we come out o' the Strait. We're bound for Corwin. Nothin' contraband. All reg'lar. Six hunters, two damaged in the gale, though the doc's fixed 'em up. Twelve seamen, one boy, an' a nigger cook who's pizened himself with his own cookin'. Doc's bringin' him round, too, though he don't deserve it. Want to make yore inspection? We're in no hurry to git away until the ice melts. Take yore time."

The little, dapper officer with his keen, high-cheeked face, and his shoe-brush hair, got up and bowed, with a side glance at Peggy Simms.

"It is not usual for young ladies to be so far north." His endeavor at gallantry was obvious.

"I am with my father," said the girl, looking at Rainey, enjoying the situation.

"Where I go she goes," said Lund. And looked in turn at her with relish in his double suggestion. He, too, was playing the game, gambling, believing in his luck, reckless, now he had set the board.

They passed through the corridor. Lund opened up the strong-room, and then the galley. It was orderly, and there was a moaning figure in Tamada's bunk, a tossing figure with a head bound in a red bandanna above the black face and neck that showed above the blankets. The eyes were closed. The black hands, showing lighter palms, plucked at the coverings.

"Delirious," said Lund. "Serves him right. He's a rotten cook."

"Have you all the medicines you need?" asked Ito. "I can send our surgeon."

"I can manage," returned Rainey, *alias* Carlsen. "It's enteric. I've reduced the fever."

They passed on through the hunters' quarters. The girl fell behind with Rainey.

"A good make-up and a good actor," she whispered. "I helped him to be sure he covered everything that would show. It was my idea about the bandanna. Just what a sick negro might wear, and it hid his straight hair."

The lieutenant appeared fairly satisfied, but requested that Lund go on board his ship. He stayed there until sundown, returning in hilarious mood.

"We've slipped it over on 'em this time," he said. "I left 'em aswim with *sake*, an' bubblin' over with polite regrets. But they'll be back in three weeks, they said, if the ice is open. An', if the luck holds, we'll be out of it. I don't want them searchin' the ship ag'in." He slapped Tamada on the back as he came to serve supper after Sandy had laid the table.

"A reg'lar vodeville skit," he exclaimed. "You're some actor, Tamada! But why didn't you say the island was down on their charts? They've even got a name for it. Hiyama."

"It means hot mountain," said Tamada. "The government names many islands."

"You can bet yore life they do," said Lund. "They're smart, but they overlooked that beach an' they've given us three weeks to cash in."

Lund himself had imbibed enough of the *sake* to make him loose of tongue, added to his elation at the success he had achieved. The gunboat was gone on its patrol, and he had a free hand. He half filled a glass with whisky. "Here's to luck," he cried. And spilled a part of the liquor on the floor before he set the glass to his lips.

"Here's to you, Doc," he added. "An' to Peggy!" He rolled eyes that were a trifle bloodshot at the girl.

"Our relations have gone back as usual, Mr. Lund," she said quietly. Lund glared at her half truculently.

"I'm agreeable," he said. "As a daughter, I disown you from now on, Miss Peggy. Here's to ye, jest the same!"

CHAPTER XVII
MY MATE

From the day following the arrival and departure of the Japanese gunboat, they attacked the little U-shaped beach that lay between two buttresses of the volcano and sloped sharply down to the sea. Twenty-one men, a lad and a woman, they went at the despoiling of it with a sort of obsession, led, rather than driven, by Lund, who worked among the rest of them like a Hercules.

From the beginning the tongue of shingle promised to be almost incredibly rich. Between these two spurs of mountain the tide had washed and flung the rich, free-flaking gold of a submarine vein, piling it up for unguessable years. Ebb tides had worked it in among the gravel, floods had beaten it down; the deeper they went to bedrock, the richer the pan.

The men's fancy estimate of a million dollars began speedily to seem small as the work progressed, systematically stripping the rocky floor of all its shingle, foot by foot, and cubic yard by cubic yard, cradling it in crude rockers, fluming it, vaporizing the amalgam of gold and mercury, and adding pound after pound of virgin gold to the sacks in the schooner's strong-room.

They worked at first in alternating shifts of four hours, by day and night, under the sun, the moon, the stars and the flaming aurora. The crust was drilled here and there where it had frozen into conglomerate, and exploded by dynamite, carefully placed so as not to dislodge the masses of ice that overhung the schooner. Fires to thaw out the ground were unavailable for sheer lack of fuel; there was no driftwood between these forestless shores. What fuel could be spared was conserved for use under the boilers that melted ice to provide water for the cradles and flumes, and help to cook the meals that Tamada prepared out-of-doors for the workers.

Buckets of coffee, stews, and thick soups of peas and lentils, masses of beans with plenty of fat pork, these were what they craved after hours of tremendous endeavor. Despite the cold, they sweated profusely at their tasks, stripping off over-garments as they picked and shoveled or crowbarred out the rich gravel.

Peggy Simms worked with the rest, assisting Tamada, helping to serve with Sandy. Deming, and Beale, the man with the damaged ribs, were given odd jobs that they could handle: feeding the fires, washing up, or assisting at the little forge where the drills were sharpened.

Through all of it Lund was supreme as working superintendent. There was no job that he could not, did not, handle better than any two of them, and, though Rainey could see a shrinkage, or a compression, of his bulk as day by day he called upon it for heroic service, he never seemed to tire.

"Got to keep 'em at it," he would say in the cabin. "No time to lose, an' the odds all against us, in a way. Barring Luck. That's what we got to count on, but we don't want them thinkin' that. If the weather don't break — an' break jest right — as soon as we've cleaned up, we're stung. Though I'll blast a way out of this shore ice, if it comes to the worst. I saved out some dynamite on purpose."

"We ought to have brought a steam-shovel along," said Rainey. He was hard as iron, but he had served a tough apprenticeship to labor, and his hands and nails, he fancied, would never get into shape again.

"Now you're talkin'," agreed Lund. "We c'ud have handled it in fine shape an' left the machine behind as junk or a souvenir for our Jap friends. We've got to cut out this four-hour shift. Too much time wasted changin'. Too many meals. We'll make it one long, steady shift of all hands long as we can stand up to it, an' all git reg'lar sleep. I'm needin' some myself."

Rainey knew that neither he nor Hansen got within two-thirds as much out of their shifts as when Lund was in command, though he had given them the pick of the men. It was not that the men malingered, they simply, neither of them, had the knack of keeping the work going at top speed and top effectiveness.

But, with Lund handling all of them as a unit, it was not long before the shovels began to scrape on the bare rock that underlay the gravel at tide edge, and work swiftly back to the end of the U. The outdoors kitchen had been established on top of the promontory between the schooner and the beach, a primitive arrangement of big pots slung from tripods over fires kindled on a flat area that was partly sheltered from the sea and the prevailing winds by outcrops of weathered lava.

At dawn the men trooped from the schooner to be fed and warmed, and then they flung themselves at their task. The more they got out the more there was in it for them. But Lund was their overlord, their better, and they knew it. Only Deming worked with one hand the handle of the forge bellows, or fed the fires, and sneered.

Lund stood a full head above the tallest of them, which was Rainey, and he was always in the thick of the work, directing, demanding the utmost, and setting example to back command. His eyes had bothered him, and he had made a pair of Arctic snow-glasses, mere circles of wood with slits in them. But under these the sweat gathered, and he discarded them, resorting to the primitive device of smearing soot all about his eyes. This, he said, gave him relief, but it made him a weird sort of Caliban in his labors.

On the fifteenth day, with the work better than half done, with more than a ton of actual gold in colors, that ranged from flour dust to nuggets, in the strong-room, the weather began to change. It misted continually, and Lund, rejoicing, prophesied the breaking up of the cold snap.

By the eighteenth day a regular Chinook was blowing, melting the sharper outlines of the icy crags and pinnacles, and providing streams of moisture that, in the nights now gradually growing longer, glazed every yard of rock with peril.

The men worked in a muck with their rubber sea-boots worn out by constant chafing, sweaters torn, the blades of their shovels reduced by the work demanded of them, the drills, shortened by steady sharpening, gone like the spare flesh of the laborers, who, at last, began to show signs of quicker and quicker exhaustion with occasional mutterings of discontent, while Lund, intent only upon cleaning off the rock as a dentist cleans a crumbling tooth, coaxed and cursed, blamed and praised and bullied, and did the actual work of three of them.

Dead with fatigue, filled with food, drowsy from the liberal grog allowance at the end of the day, the men slept in a torpor every night and showed less and less inclination to respond, though the end of their labors was almost in sight.

"What's the use, we got enough," was the comment beginning to be heard more and more frequently. "Lund, he's got more'n he can spend in a lifetime!"

Rainey could not trace these mutterings to Deming's instigation, but he suspected the hunter. There was no poker; all hands were too tired for play.

The ice in which the schooner was packed began to show signs of disintegration. The surface rotted by day and froze again by night and this destroyed its compactness. If the sun's arc above the horizon had been longer, its rays more vertical, the ice must infallibly have melted and freed the *Karluk*, for it was salt-water ice, and there were times when the thermometer stayed above its freezing point for two or three hours around noon.

Lund gave the holding floe scant attention. So long as the present weather kept up he declared that he could dynamite his way out inside of four hours.

The effect of all this on Rainey was a bit bewildering. He was judging life by new standards far apart from his own modes and, though he, too, worked with a will, and rejoiced in the freer effort of his muscles, the result comparing favorably with the best of the others — save Lund — he could not assimilate the general conditions.

They were too purely physical, he told himself; he missed his old habits, the reading and discussion of books, new and old, the good restaurants of San Francisco, and the chat he had been used to hold over their tables, companionable, witty, the exchange and stimulation of ideas.

He missed the theaters, the concerts, the passing show of well-dressed women, a hodge-podge of flesh-pots and mental uplift. He got to dreaming of these things nights.

Daytimes, he saw plainly that, in this environment at least, Lund was big, and the rest of them comparatively small. He believed that Lund could actually form a little kingdom of his own, as he had suggested, and make a success of it. But it would not be a kingdom that fostered the arts. It would cultivate the sciences, or at least encourage them and adopt results as applied to land development, and, if necessary, the defense of the kingdom.

Lund would be a figure in war and peace, peace of the practical sort, the kind of peace that went with plenty. He was no dreamer, but a utilitarian. Perhaps, after all, the world most needed such men just now.

As for Peggy Simms, she did not lose the polish of her culture, she was always feminine, even dainty at times, despite her work, that could not help but be coarse to a certain extent. She was full of vigor, she showed unexpected strength, she was a source of encouragement to the men as she waited on them. And also a source of undisguised admiration, all of which she shed as a duck sheds water. She was filled with abounding health, she moved with a free grace that held the eye and lingered in the mind. She was eminently a woman, and she also was big.

Rainey gained an increasing respect in her prowess, and a swift conversion to the equality of the sexes. There were times when he doubted his own equality. Had she met him on his own ground, in his own realm of what he considered vaguely as culture, he would have known a mastery that he now lacked. As it was, she averaged higher, and she had an attraction of sex that was compelling.

Here was a girl who would demand certain standards in the man with whom she would mate, not merely accompany through life. There were times when Rainey felt irresistibly the charm of her as a woman, longed for her in the powerful sex reactions that inevitably follow hard labor. There were times when he felt that she did not consider that he measured up to her gages, and he would strive to change the atmosphere, to dominate the situation in which Lund was the greater figure of the two men.

The rivalry that Lund had suggested between them as regards the girl, Rainey felt almost thrust upon him. There were moods which Peggy Simms turned to him for sharing, but there was scant time in the waking hours for love-making, or even its consideration.

Lund was centered on one achievement, the gold harvest. He ordered the girl with the rest; there were even times when he reprimanded her, while Rainey burned with the resentment she apparently did not share.

A little before dawn on the eighteenth day of the work upon the beach, Lund was out upon the floe examining the condition of the ice. He had declared that two days more of hard endeavor would complete their labors. What dirt remained at the end of that time they would transship. Rainey had joined the girl and Tamada at the cook fires.

The sky was bright with the aurora borealis that would pale before the sun. The men were not yet out of their bunks. They were bone and muscle tired, and Rainey doubted whether Lund, gaunt and lean himself, could get two days of top work out of them. Near the fires for the cooking, the melting of water and the forge, that were kept glowing all night, the tools were stacked, to help preserve their temper.

The aurora quivered in varying incandescence as Rainey watched Lund prodding at the floe ice with a steel bar. The girl was busy with the coffee, and Tamada was compounding two pots of stew and bubbling peas pudding for the breakfast, food for heat and muscle making.

Sandy appeared on deck and came swiftly over the side of the vessel and up the worn trail to the fires. He showed excitement, Rainey fancied, sure of it as the lad got within speaking distance.

"Where is Mr. Lund?" he panted.

Rainey pointed to Lund, now examining a crack that had opened up in the floe, a possible line of exit for the *Karluk*, later on. The men were beginning to show on the schooner. They, too, he noted somewhat idly, acted differently this morning. Usually they were sluggish until they had eaten, sleepy and indifferent until the coffee stimulated them, and Lund took up this stimulus and fanned it to a flame of work. This morning they walked differently, abnormally active.

"They're drunk, an' they're goin' on strike," said Sandy. "You know the big demijohn in the lazaretto?"

Rainey nodded. It was a two-handled affair holding five gallons, a reserve supply of strong rum from which Lund dispensed the grog allowances and stimulations for extra work toward the end of the shift, the night-caps and occasional rewards.

"They've swiped it," he said. "Put an empty one from the hold in its place. We got plenty without usin' that one for a while, an' I only happened to notice it this morning by chance. They've bin drinkin' all night, I reckon. They're ugly, Mr. Rainey. It's the crew this time. They got the booze. The hunters are sober. Deming ain't in on this. They did it on their own. I don't know how they got it. I didn't get it for 'em, sir. They must have worked plumb through the hold an' got to it that way."

"All right, Sandy. Thanks. Mr. Lund can handle them, I guess. He's coming now."

The men had got to the ice, hidden from Lund, who was walking to the *Karluk* on the opposite side of the vessel. The seamen were gesticulating freely; the sound of their voices came up to him where he stood, tinged with a new freedom of speech, rough, confident, menacing. As they climbed the trail their legs betrayed them and confirmed the boy's story. Behind them came the four hunters, with Hansen, walking apart, watching the sailors with a certain gravity that communicated itself despite the distance.

Lund showed at the far rail of the schooner with his bar. He glanced toward the men going to work, went below, and came up with a sweater. He had left the bar behind him in the cabin, where it was used for a stove poker.

The men filed by Rainey, their faces flushed and their eyes unusually bright. They seemed to share a prime joke that wanted to bubble up and over, yet held a restraint upon themselves that was eased by digs in one another's ribs, in laughs when one stumbled or hiccoughed.

But Hansen was stolid as ever, and the hunters had evidently not shared the stolen liquor. Only Deming's eyes roved over the group of men as they gathered round for their cups and pannikins of food. He seemed to be calculating what advantage he could gain out of this unexpected happening.

Peggy Simms, under cover of pouring the coffee, sweetened heavily with condensed milk, found time to speak to Rainey.

"They're all drunk," she said.

"Not all of them. Here comes Lund. He'll handle it."

Lund seemed still pondering the problem of the floe. At first he did not notice the condition of the sailors. Then he apparently ignored it. But, after they had eaten, he talked to all the men.

"Two more days of it, lads, and we're through. The beach is nigh cleared. We can git out of the floe to blue water easy enough, an' we'll git a good start on the patrol-ship. We'll go back with full pockets an' heavy ones. The shares'll be half as large again as we've figgered. I wouldn't wonder if they averaged sixteen or seventeen thousand dollars apiece."

Rainey had picked out a black-bearded Finn as the leader of the sailors in their debauch. The liquor seemed to have unchained in him a spirit of revolt that bordered on insolence. He stood with his bowed legs apart, mittened hands on hips, staring at Lund with a covert grin.

Next to Lund he was the biggest man aboard. With the rum giving an unusual coordination to his usually sluggish nervous system, he promised to be a source of trouble.

Rainey was surprised to see him shrug his shoulders and lead the way to the beach. Perhaps breakfast had sobered them, though the fumes of liquor still clung cloudily on the air.

Lund went down, with Rainey beside him, reporting Sandy.

"I'll work it out of 'em," said Lund. "That booze'll be an expensive luxury to 'em, paid for in hard labor."

They found the men ranged up in three groups. Deming and Beale, against custom, had gone down to the beach. They were supposed to help clean the food utensils, and aid Tamada after a meal, besides replenishing the fires.

They stood a little away from the hunters and Hansen and the sailors. The Finn, talking to his comrades in a low growl, was with a separate group.

There was an air of defiance manifest, a feeling of suspense in the tiny valley, backed by the frowning cone, ribbed by the two icy promontories. Lund surveyed them sharply.

"What in hell's the matter with you?" he barked. "Hansen, send up a man for the drills an' shovels. Yore work's laid out; hop to it!"

"We ain't goin' to work no more," said the Finn aggressively. "Not fo' no sich wage like you give."

"Oh, you ain't, ain't you?" mocked Lund. He was standing with Rainey in the middle of the space they had cleared of gravel, the seamen lower down the beach, nearer the sea, their ranks compacted. "Why, you booze-bitten, lousy hunky, what in hell do you want? You never saw twenty dollars in a lump you c'u'd call yore own for more'n ten minnits. You boardin'-house loafer an' the rest of you scum o' the seven seas, git yore shovels an' git to diggin', or I'll put you ashore in San Francisco flat broke, an' glad to leave the ship, at that. *Jump!*"

The Finn snarled, and the rest stood firm. Not one of them knew the real value of their promised share. Money represented only counters exchanged for lodging, food and drink enough to make them sodden before they had spent even their usual wages. Then they would wake to find the rest gone, and throw themselves upon the selfish bounty of a boarding-house keeper.

But they had seen the gold, they had handled it, and they were inflamed by a sense of what it ought to do for them. Perhaps half of them could not add a simple sum, could not grasp figures beyond a thousand, at most. And the sight of so much gold had made it, in a manner, cheap. It was there, a heap of it, and they wanted more of that shining heap than had been promised them.

"You talk big," said the Finn. "Look my hands." He showed palms calloused, split, swollen lumps of chilblained flesh worn down and stiffened. "I bin seaman, not goddam navvy."

Lund turned to the hunters.

"You in on this?" he asked. Deming and Beale moved off. Two of the others joined them. "Neutral?" sneered Lund. "I'll remember that." Hansen and the two remaining came over beside Lund and Rainey.

"Five of us," said Lund. "Five men against twelve fo'c'sle rats. I'll give you two minnits to start work."

"You talk big with yore gun in pocket," said the Finn. "Me good man as you enny day."

Lund's face turned dark with a burst of rage that exploded in voice and action.

"You think I need my gun, do ye, you pack of rats? Then try it on without it."

His hand slid to his holster inside his heavy coat. His arm swung, there was a streak of gleaming metal in the lifting sun-rays, flying over the heads of the seamen. It plunked in the free water beyond the ice.

"Come on," roared Lund, "or I'll rush you to the first bath you've had in five years." The Finn lowered his head, and charged; the rest followed their leader. The hot food had steadied their motive control to a certain extent, they were firmer on their feet, less vague of eye, but the crude alcohol still fumed in their brains. Without it they would never have answered the Finn's call to rebellion.

He had promised, and their drunken minds believed, that refusing in a mass to work would automatically halt things until they got their "rights." They had not expected an open fight. The spur of alcohol had thrust them over the edge, given them a swifter flow of their impoverished blood, a temporary confidence in their own prowess, a mock valor that answered Lund's contemptuous challenge.

Lund, thought Rainey, had done a foolhardy thing in tossing away his gun. It was magnificent, but it was not war. Pure bravado! But he had scant time for thinking. Lund tossed him a scrap of advice. "Keep movin'! Don't let 'em crowd you!" Then the fight was joined.

The girl leaned out from the promontory to watch the tourney. Tamada, impassive as ever, tended his fires. Sandy crept down to the beach, drawn despite his will, and shuffled in and out, irresolute, too weak to attempt to mix in, but excited, eager to help. Deming, Beale, and the two neutral hunters, stood to one side, waiting, perhaps, to see which way the fight went, reserves for the apparent victor.

The Finn, best and biggest of the sailors, rushed for Lund, his little eyes red with rage, crazy with the desire to make good his boast that he was as good as Lund. In his barbaric way he was somewhat of a dancer, and his legs were as lissome as his arms. He leaped, striking with fists and feet.

Lund met him with a fierce upper-cut, short-traveled, sent from the hip. His enormous hand, bunched to a knuckly lump of stone, knocked the Finn over, lifting him, before he fell with his nose driven in, its bone shattered, his lips broken like overripe fruit, and his discolored teeth knocked out.

He landed on his back, rolling over and over, to lie still, half stunned, while two more sprang for Lund.

Lund roared with surprise and pain as one caught his red beard and swung to it, smiting and kicking. He wrapped his left arm about the man, crushing him close up to him, and, as the other came, diving low, butting at his solar plexus, the giant gripped him by the collar, using his own impetus, and brought the two skulls together with a thud that left them stunned.

The two dropped from Lund's relaxed arms like sacks, and he stepped over them, alert, poised on the balls of his feet, letting out a shout of triumph, while he looked about him for his next adversary.

The bedrock on which they fought was slippery where ice had formed in the crevices. Two seamen tackled Hansen. He stopped the curses of one with a straight punch to his mouth, but the man clung to his arm, bearing it down. Hansen swung at the other, and the blow went over the shoulder as he dodged, but Hansen got him in chancery, and the three, staggering, swearing, sliding, went down at last together, with Hansen underneath, twisting one's neck to shut off his wind while he warded off the wild blows of the second. With a wild heave he got on all-fours, and then Lund, roaring like a bull as he came, tore off a seaman and flung him headlong.

"Pound him, Hansen!" he shouted, his eyes hard with purpose, shining like ice that reflects the sun, his nostrils wide, glorying in the fight.

The Finn had got himself together a bit, wiping the gouts of blood from his face and spitting out the snags of his broken teeth. He drew a knife from inside his shirt, a long, curving blade, and sidled, like a crab, toward Lund, murder in his piggy, bloodshot eyes, waiting for a chance to slip in and stab Lund in the back, calling to a comrade to help him.

"Come on," he called, "Olsen, wit' yore knife. Gut the swine!"

Another blade flashed out, and the pair advanced, crouching, knees and bodies bent. Lund backed warily toward the opposite cliff, looking for a loose rock fragment. He had forbidden knives to the sailors since the mutiny, and had forced a delivery, but these two had been hidden. A knife to the Finn was a natural accessory. Only his drunken frenzy had made him try to beat Lund at his own game.

One of the two hunters, lamed with a kick on the knee, howling with the pain, clinched savagely and bore the seaman down, battering his head against a knob of rock. The other friendly hunter had bashed and buffeted his opponent to submission. But Rainey was in hard case.

A seaman, half Mexican, flew at him like a wildcat. Rainey struck out, and his fists hit at the top of the breed's head without stopping him. Then he clinched.

The Mexican was slippery as an eel. He got his arms free, his hands shot up, and his thumbs sought the inner corners of Rainey's eyes. The sudden, burning anguish was maddening and he drove his clasped fists upward, wedging away the drilling fingers.

Two hands clawed at his shoulders from behind. Some one sprang fairly on his back. A knee thrust against his spine.

The agony left him helpless, the vertebræ seemed about to crack. Strength and will were shut off, and the world went black. And then one of the hunters catapulted into the struggle, and the four of them went down in a maddened frenzy of blows and stifled shouts.

The sailors fought like beasts, striving for blows barred by all codes of decency and fair play, intent to maim. Lund had got his shoulders against the rocks and stood with open hands, watching the two with their knives, who crept in, foot by foot, to make a finish.

Peggy Simms, a strand of her pale yellow hair whipped loose, flung it out of her eyes as she stood on the edge of the cliff, her lips apart, her breasts rising stormily, watching; her features changing with the tide of battle as it surged beneath her, punctuated with muffled shouts and wind-clipped oaths. She saw Lund at bay, and snatched out her pistol. But the distance was too great. She dared not trust her aim.

Sandy, dancing in and out, willing but helpless, bound by fear and lack of muscle, saw Deming, followed by Beale, stealing up the trail, unnoticed by the girl, who leaned far forward, watching the fight, her eyes on Lund and the two creeping closer with their knives, cautious but determined. Tamada stood farther back and could not see them.

The lad's wits, sharpened by his forecastle experience, surmised what Deming and Beale were after as they gained the promontory flat and ran toward the fires.

"Hey!" he shrilled. "Look out; they're after the tools!"

Deming's hand was stretched toward a shovel, its worn steel scoop sharp as a chisel. Beale was a few feet behind him. They were going to toss the shovels and drills down to the seamen.

Tamada turned. His face did not change, but his eyes gleamed as he thrust a dipper in the steaming remnants of the pea-soup and flung the thick blistering mass fair in Deming's face. At the same moment the girl's pistol cracked with a stab of red flame. Beale dropped, shot in the neck, close to the collarbone, twisting like a scotched snake, rolling down the trail to the beach again.

Deming, howling like a scorched devil, clawed with one hand at the sticky mass that masked him as he ran blind, wild with pain. He tripped, clutched, and lost his hold, slid on a plane of icy lava, smooth as glass, struck a buttress that sent him off at a tangent down the face of the cliff, bounding from impact with an outthrust elbow of the rock, whirling into space, into the icy turmoil of the waves, flooding into the inlet.

Peggy Simms fled down the trail with a steel drill in either hand, straight across the beach toward Lund. The Finn turned on her with a snarl and a side-swipe of his knife, but she leaped aside, dodged the other slow-foot, and thrust a drill at Lund, who grasped it with a cry of exultation, swinging it over his head as if it had been a bamboo. Hansen had shaken off his men, and came leaping in for the second drill.

The knife fell tinkling on the frozen rock as Lund smashed the wrist of the Finn. The girl's gun made the second would-be stabber throw up his hands while Hansen snatched his weapon, flung it over the farther cliff, and knocked the seaman to the ground before he joined Lund, charging the rest, who fled before the sight of them and the threat of the bars of steel.

Lund laughed loud, and stopped striking, using the drill as a goad, driving them into a huddled horde, like leaderless sheep, knee-deep, thigh-deep, into the water, where they stopped and begged for mercy while Hansen turned to put a finish to the separate struggles.

It ended as swiftly as it had begun. One hunter could barely stand for his kicked knee, Rainey's back was strained and stiffening, Lund had lost a handful of his beard, and Hansen's cheek was laid open.

On the other side the casualties were more severe. Deming was drowned, his body flung up by the tide, rolling in the swash. Beale was coughing blood, though not dangerously wounded. The Finn was crying over his broken wrist, all the fight out of him. Ribs were sore where not splintered from the drills, and the two bumped by Lund sat up with sorely aching heads. The courage inspired by the liquor was all gone; oozed, beaten out of them. They were cowed, demoralized, whipped.

Lund took swift inventory, lining them up as they came timorously out of the water or straggled against the cliff at his order. Tamada had come down from the fires. Peggy had told of his share, and Sandy's timely shout. Lund nodded at him in a friendly manner.

"You're a white man, Tamada," he said. "You, too, Sandy. I'll not forget it. Rainey, round up these derelicts an' help Tamada fix 'em up. I'll settle with 'em later. Hansen, put the rest of 'em to work, an' keep 'em to it! Do you hear? They got to do the work of the whole bunch."

They went willingly enough, limping, nursing their bruises, while Hansen, his stolidity momentarily vanished in the rush of the fight and not yet regained, exhibited an unusual vocabulary as he bossed them. Lund turned to the two hunters, who had stood apart.

"Wal, you yellow-bellied neutrals," he said, his voice cold and his eyes hard. "Thought I might lose, and hoped so, didn't you? Pick up that skunk Beale an' tote him aboard. Then come back an' go to work. You'll git yore shares, but you'll not git what's comin' to those who stood by. Now git out of my sight. You can bury That when you come back." He nodded at the sodden corpse of Deming, flung up on the grit. "You can take yore pay as grave-diggers out of what you owe him at poker. He ain't goin' to collect this trip."

Rainey, lame and sore, helped Tamada patch up the wounded, turning the hunters' quarters into a sick bay, using the table for operation. Beale was the worst off, but Tamada pronounced him not vitally damaged. After he had finished with them he insisted upon Rainey's lying, face down, on the table, stripped to the waist, while he rubbed him with oil and then kneaded him. Once he gave a sudden, twisting wrench, and Rainey saw a blur of stars as something snapped into place with a click.

"I think you soon all right, now," said Tamada.

"You and Miss Simms turned the tide," said Rainey. "If they'd got those tools first they'd have finished us in short order."

"Fools!" said Tamada. "Suppose they kill Lund, how they get away? No one to navigate. Presently the gunboat would find them. I think Mr. Lund will maybe trust me now," he said quietly.

"What do you mean?"

"Mr. Lund think in the back of his head I arrange for that gunboat to come. He can not understand how they know the schooner at island. He think to come jus' this time too much curious, I think."

"It was a bit of a coincidence."

Tamada shrugged his shoulders slightly.

"I think Japanese government know all that goes on in North Polar region," he said. "There is wireless station on Wrangell Island. We pass by that pretty close."

Rainey chewed that information as he put on his clothes, wondering if they had seen the last of the gunboat. They would have to pass south through Bering Strait. It would be easy to overhaul them, halt them, search the schooner, confiscate the gold. They were not out of trouble yet.

When he went into the cabin to replace his torn coat — he had hardly a button intact above the waist, from jacket to undershirt — he found the girl there with Lund. Apparently, they had just come in. Peggy Simms, with face aglow with the excitement that had not subsided, was proffering Lund her pistol.

"Keep it," he said. "You may need it. I've got mine."

"But you threw it into the water. I saw you."

"No," He laughed. "That wasn't my gun. They thought it was. I wanted to bring the thing to grips. But I wasn't fool enough to chuck away my gun. That was a wrench I was usin' this mornin' to fix the cabin stove — looks jest like an ottermatic. I stuck it in my inside pocket. I was ha'f a mind to shoot when they showed their knives, but I didn't want to use my gun on that mess of hash."

He stood tall and broad above her, looking down at the face that was raised to his. Rainey, unnoticed as yet, saw her eyes bright with admiration.

"You are a wonderful fighter," she said softly.

"Wonderful? What about you? A man's woman! You saved the day. Comin' to me with them drills. An' we licked 'em. We. God!"

He swept her up into his arms, lifting her in his big hands, making no more of her than if she had been a feather pillow, up till her face was on a level with his, pressing her close, while in swift, indignant rage she fought back at him, striking futilely while he held her, kissed her, and set her down as Rainey sprang forward.

Lund seemed utterly unconscious of the girl's revulsion.

"Comin' to me with the drills!" he said. "We licked 'em. You an' me together. My woman!"

Peggy Simms had leaped back, her eyes blazing. Lund came for her, his face lit with the desire of her, arms outspread, hands open. Before Rainey could fling himself between them, the girl had snatched the little pistol that Lund had set on the table and fired point-blank. She seemed to have missed, though Lund halted, his mouth agape, astounded.

"You big bully!" said Rainey. Now that the time had come he found that he was not afraid of Lund, of his gun, of his strength. "Play fair, do you? Then show it! You asked me once why I didn't make love to her. I told you. But you, you foul-minded bully! All you think of is your big body, to take what it wants.

"Peggy. Will you marry me? I can protect you from this hulking brute. If it's to be a show-down between you and me," he flared at Lund, still gazing as if stupefied, "let it come now. Peggy?"

The girl, tears on her cheeks that were born from the sobs of anger that had shaken her, swung on him.

"You?" she said, and Rainey wilted under the scorn in her voice. "Marry you?" She began to laugh hysterically, trying to check herself.

"I didn't mean you enny harm," said Lund slowly, addressing Peggy. "Why, I wouldn't harm you, gal. You're my woman. You come to me. I was jest — jest sorter swept off my bearin's. Why," he turned to Rainey, his voice down-pitching to a growl of angry contempt, "you pen-shovin' whippersnapper, I c'ud break you in ha'f with one hand. You ain't her breed. But" — his voice changed again — "if it's a show-down, all right.

"If I was to fight you, over her, I'd kill you. D'ye think I don't respect a good gal? D'ye think I don't know how to love a gal right? She's *my* mate. Not yours. But it's up to you, Peggy Simms. I didn't mean to insult you. An' if you want him — why, it's up to you to choose between the two of us."

She went by Rainey as if he had not existed, straight into Lund's arms, her face radiant, upturned.

"It's you I love, Jim Lund," she said. "A man. *My* man."

As her arms went round his neck she gave a little cry.

"I wounded you," she said, and the tender concern of her struck Rainey to the quick. "Quick, let me see."

"Wounded, hell!" laughed Lund. "D'ye think that popgun of yores c'ud stop me? The pellet's somewheres in my shoulder. Let it bide. By God, yo're my woman, after all. Lund's Luck!"

Rainey went up on deck with that ringing in his ears. His humiliation wore off swiftly as he crossed back toward the beach. By the time he crossed the promontory he even felt relieved at the outcome. He was not in love with her. He had known that when he intervened. He had not even told her so. His chivalry had spoken — not his heart. And his thoughts strayed back to California. The other girl, Diana though she was, would never, in almost one breath, have shot and kissed the man she loved. A lingering vision of Peggy Simms' beauty as she had gone to Lund remained and faded.

"Lund's right," he told himself. "She's not of my breed."

CHAPTER XVIII
LUND'S LUCK

Lund glanced at the geyser of spray where the shell from the pursuing gunboat had fallen short, and then at the bank of mist ahead. They were in the narrows of Bering Strait, between the Cape of Charles and Prince Edward's Point, the gold aboard, a full wind in their sails, making eleven knots to the gunboat's fifteen.

It was mid-afternoon, three hours since they had seen smoke to the north and astern of them. Either the patrol had found them gone from the island, freed by blasting from the floe, and followed on the trail full speed, or the wireless from some Japanese station on the Tchukchis coast had told of their homing flight.

The great curtain of fog was a mile ahead. The last shell had fallen two hundred yards short. Five minutes more would settle it. Hansen had the wheel. Lund stood by the taffrail, his arm about Peggy Simms. He shook a fist at the gunboat, vomiting black smoke from her funnel, foam about her bows.

"We'll beat 'em yet," he cried.

The next shell, with more elevation, whined parallel with them, sped ahead, and smashed into the waves.

"Hold yore course, Hansen! No time to zigzag. Got to chance it. Damn it, they know how to shoot!"

A missile had gone plump through main and foresails, leaving round holes to mark the score. Another fairly struck the main topmast, and some splinters came rattling down, while the remnants of the top-sail flapped amid writhing ends of halyard and sheet.

They entered the beginning of the fog, curling wisps of it reached out, twining over the bowsprit and headsails, enveloping the foremast, swallowing the schooner as a hurtling shell crashed into the stern. The next instant the mist had sheltered them. Lund released the girl and jumped to the wheel.

"Now then," he shouted, "we'll fool 'em!" He gripped the spokes, and the men ran to the sheets at command while the *Karluk* shot off at right angles to her previous course, skirting the fog that blanketed the wind but yet allowed sufficient breeze to filter through to give them headway, gliding like a ghost on the new tack to the east.

Rainey, tense from the explosion of the shell, jumped below at last and came back exultant.

"It was a dud, Lund!" he shouted. "Or else they didn't want to blow us up on account of the gold. But they've wrecked the cabin. The fog's coming in through the hole they made. Tamada's galley's gone. It's raked the schooner!"

"So long's it's above the water line, to hell with it! We'll make out. Listen to the fools. They've gone in after us, straight on."

The booming of the gunboat's forward battery sounded aft of them, dulled by the fog — growing fainter.

"Lund's luck! We've dodged 'em!"

"They'll be waiting for us at the passes," said Rainey. "They've got the speed on us."

"Let 'em wait. To blazes with the Aleutians! Ready again there for a tack! Sou'-east now. We'll work through this till we git to the wind ag'in. It's all blue water to the Seward Peninsula. We're bound for Nome."

"For Nome?" asked Peggy Simms.

"Nome, Peggy! An American port. The nearest harbor. An' the nearest preacher!"

THE END

9 788027 275908